A Chirstmas Spark

TO: Cissie

Happy Holidays!,

Ciara Knight

I hope you have the best holiday season. :)

Ciara Knight

Praise and Awards

USA Today Bestselling Author
Semi-finalist in the Amazon Breakthrough Novel
Contest
RONE Award Finalist
LASR Book of the Month

"Wow! My first read by Ciara Knight and all I can think of is wow!"
~Night Owl Top Pick.

"Knight does a fantastic job keeping readers intrigued throughout..."
~RT Book Reviews, 4 Stars.

A Christmas Spark – Sweetwater County Series
Ciara Knight
ISBN-13: 978-1-939081-43-8

© Ciara Knight 2015. All rights reserved.
Cover Art: Robin Ludwig
Editor: Cora Artz

May you find your Christmas Spark.

CHAPTER ONE

The twisty mountain road took a sharp right and Sara Foster's BMW fishtailed on the slick asphalt.

The traction control light flickered faster than her heartbeat hammering in her chest.

She gripped the steering wheel tight and eyed the road ahead. If she could trust her childhood memory, there'd be a country store around the next bend. More memories threatened to invade through the small window she'd opened into her past, but she slammed it shut and took the next turn slow and steady. The jagged rock wall to her right blocked her view until she rounded the last bend and spotted the small wooden sign a few hundred yards ahead. *Last Stop Mom and Pop Shop.*

The flash of a former life invaded her brain sealing her breath inside her lungs. Christmas morning. Mother crying. Sara rocking with her baby sister on her lap in the cold. Red and blue lights flash on the tree.

She shook her head and flipped on her turn signal before guiding her car into the small parking lot in front of the store. A Christmas sale sign hung over garden gnomes with Santa hats. The view through her windshield was an exact match to the image in her head, as though time had frozen. The same gaudy neon sign, the cute totem pole bears, and *those* rockers.

The drizzle morphed into sleet, sealing her fate on the mountain, and her sister's anger when she learned Sara wouldn't make it for Christmas Eve dinner. She eyed the phone, but decided to face the icy wind instead of her sister's frosty tone.

With her hood slung over her head, Sara trudged through the muck to the front porch. The rocker closest to the door moved back and forth in the wind, as if the ghost of her former self sat watching her, warning her not to go up the mountain. To not return to her past. To not face her worst nightmare.

The cold chased her from her thoughts and into the small store. Fresh coffee, cinnamon, and something that smelled like cloves welcomed her, making her dread leaving all the more. Like an oasis, the shop was the last stop before her treacherous drive to the cabin on the mountain's ridge.

"Welcome!" an older lady called from the back, with the gravelly voice of a seasoned smoker. "Help yourself to some hot cocoa while you shop. Best to warm your bones after being out in that mess." The thin woman with a straight back and firm wrinkled brow stopped a few feet away. A Smokey-the-Bear-looking-for-fire stare traveled from Sara's head to her toes and back. "You from 'round here, darlin'?"

Sara retrieved a small wicker shopping basket and hung it from the crook of her arm. "No, ma'am. I haven't been to Haven Mountain since I was a little girl." Some name, that ridge had been anything but a haven in her childhood. She moved to the large commercial refrigerator and picked up a half gallon of milk, some cream then went to the canned goods. Each click of her heels against the hardwood floors echoed hauntingly in the small space. A strange feeling, a ghost of a previous life shadowed her around the store. Or perhaps it was the old lady only a few steps behind, still gawking at her.

"Hmmm. I never forget a face. Of course, I don't see many new ones 'round here. That's why I remember all 'em that pass through 'ere." The lady swished her lips back and forth like a toothless mule.

Sara didn't respond. No need to get into a long conversation when she had no intention of ever stopping by here again. The roads were getting worse by the minute, and she needed to reach the cabin before they became impassable and she was forced to return to town and face another Christmas with her sister's happy family, and the inevitable blind date she'd have waiting at the Christmas table. This year it was Dalton. A man she felt like she already knew with all that Susan had told her about him. She'd be the worst date ever this Christmas. If nothing else, she was sparing the poor guy from her mopey disposition. There was nothing to celebrate, with a failed marriage and her son spending Christmas in New York City.

"I do know you. Those bright blue eyes...like a cloudless sky, and that doll-like pale skin. Yes. I know you."

Sara tucked her chin to her chest and passed the woman, not wanting to give her a better look, but the woman trotted after her. Cereal, bread, peanut butter and jelly, and a few other items she tossed in for good measure that would get her through the next few days. She plopped the basket and extra items on the front counter and pulled out her wallet.

"Not much. Guess you're not staying more than a spell." The woman clicked her fingers against the old-fashioned cash register, but her gaze kept popping to Sara. A twinge of unease scrunched her insides tight. She flipped open her wallet and retrieved her credit card.

"Cash only." The lady tapped a pointed, curved nail against a sign taped to the front of the counter.

"Oh, sorry." Thank goodness she'd snagged some money from the ATM on the way out of Riverbend. She set a couple twenties down and eyed the rockers outside the door, still teetering in the wind.

"That's it. You that girl with the baby in her lap. That day. That day that...oh, darlin'. I'm so sorry. I knew I knew you, but I didn't know that was you."

Sara snatched a bag and slid her purchases into it herself, not wanting to delay her escape any further.

"Well, you turned out just fine. Guess your momma did okay after your dad died."

Sara snagged the bags and held them tight to her chest. "My mother didn't raise me. She died when I was eight. My aunt raised my sister and me, but yes, she did fine." Why'd she share that? The woman didn't need to know. She never spoke about her past or how she ended up without any parents by the age of eight. It didn't matter. Life was good, and she'd been fine.

"You goin' back up there?" the woman called after Sara.

Sara halted at the door. "Yes. Just for a couple days. We're selling the place since my aunt..." *Died.* Sara bit her lip to keep the finality of the word from escaping.

"Be careful. Roads are getting bad." The woman pointed a thin, wrinkled finger at the darkening sky outside the window.

"I'm counting on it," Sara mumbled before she thrust the door open and fled to the safety of her car. This weekend was supposed to be devoid of humans, a time for her to be alone without any words of wisdom about how she should live her life, or why she wasn't getting any younger. Or most of all, why she shouldn't reconcile with her ex.

There was only one thing she had to do before sealing the world off for a few days. She revved the engine and said, "Call Susan." The car's speakerphone repeated her words before the phone dialed.

She looked behind her despite the backup camera and reversed out of the space onto the main road. It wouldn't be long before she'd lose cell reception, which meant she could cut the conversation short.

"Hello, Sara? Are you headed over already? That's great. I think Dalton will be arriving early, too. That would give you both a chance to chat before everyone else arrives."

"I'm not headed over. Actually, I'm not going to make it to dinner tonight. I know it meant a lot to you, but I'm afraid the weather's too bad. I'm not going to be able to drive back to Riverbend."

"What do you mean? Where are you?" her sister asked, her tone harsh and scolding.

Sara took a deep breath. "I thought I'd go ahead and clear some stuff out of the cabin so we could get it sold. Unfortunately, the weather turned on me. The roads are getting slick. Perhaps tomorrow morning they'll be clear." She spoke as fast as the words would form on her lips, even though she knew there wasn't a chance based on the weather report, which she was counting on.

"The cabin? What are you doing up there? Today of all days?" Susan said, her voice screeching through the speaker like an injured owl.

"I just wanted to get it done," Sara protested.

"No, you're doing that I-failed-my-son-so-I'm-going-to-punish-myself thing."

"Listen—"

"You listen to me. It wasn't your fault. You were only a little girl. No one will ever know why dad left us on Christmas Eve because he died on the road out of town. Call it karma. But the man left us, you didn't leave your son."

"I know. I just needed to go to the cabin. I couldn't face Christmas without Josh."

"Fine, go to the cabin instead of coming here to have a nice family dinner."

"Cabin? Today? But Dalton is..." Susan's husband, Nick, sounded faraway through the speakerphone.

"What did Nick say?"

Something covered the phone and Sara could only hear muffled conversation. A moment later, Susan came back on.

"Hey, sorry. The kids needed something and, of course, Nick decided to tell me while I was on the phone with you. You know what. I think you should stay at the cabin. I guess your safety is more important than Christmas Eve dinner. You get inside the cabin and don't drive until it's safe again. Please, Sara. Promise me you'll be careful on that road."

Sara hadn't even considered how her sister would feel about her driving the same road where their father had died on Christmas Eve all those years ago. "I'm sorry. I should've thought more about—"

"Don't worry about it. You relax and come home when you can. I mentioned Dalton loves kids, right?"

Sara suppressed a sigh. "Yes, and that he's strong, handsome, involved in his church, volunteers at the animal shelter and works as a contractor and fireman. He's not lazy. He's kind-hearted and every woman's dream guy. The only thing you haven't told me is why he's divorced, doesn't have kids of his own, and is available on Christmas Eve if he's so special."

A moment of silence, something she rarely heard from her sister, made her think she'd already lost the connection. "Susan?"

"Yes, um... well, that's his story to tell. You'll have to ask him when you meet him, although I wouldn't advise leading with that as a conversation starter."

"Of course not." Sara held tight to the steering wheel, her hands at ten and two. The tires rumbled over the bridge. Once across, she relaxed but only a bit. The bridge had been nicknamed Black Ice Bridge by the locals for a reason. A fact her father had learned the hard way all those years ago.

"Well, the way you like to chase good men away I thought I should remind you."

"I don't chase men away," Sara argued. "Jack wants to reconcile, remember?"

Her sister's huff sounded more like a horse with kennel cough. "You know perfectly well that ex-husband of yours only wants your money and he's using your son to get it. I can't believe you actually agreed to see him New Year's Eve. I mean, what are you thinking? Even if you did get back together for Josh's sake, it wouldn't last. As soon as he stole all your money, he'd divorce you again. He's a—"

The speakerphone went silent, signaling the call had dropped. The only sound now, the rain tapping on the roof and her own sniffles threatening to take hold of her once again. No. She'd shed so many tears when she'd discovered Josh wanted to spend Christmas with Jack in upstate New York. How could she say no? If that was what Josh wanted, she didn't want to make him suffer because of her own selfish needs.

Christmas, a day for family and love and happiness. She wanted all that for her son, even if it meant she had nothing but sadness and loneliness. Susan was right about one thing. Jack took him to New York as a bargaining chip, to get her to agree to fly up for New Year's.

Was this really a man she wanted to be married to again? Yes, because if not, she'd be just like her father, abandoning her child for her own happiness.

CHAPTER TWO

Dalton slid his hammer into his tool belt and took a swig of coffee before donning his heavy coat. The landline shrilled in the small space, sending Pepper diving for cover under the brown and orange plaid sofa. "It's okay, boy."

The poor black lab had been abused by some previous owner. The minute Dalton spotted him in the shelter he knew he had to bring him home.

He reached for the phone as it rang once more, followed by Pepper's whining.

Dalton squatted and eyed the shaking animal. "Hello?"

"Hey, man. It's Nick. I thought you might be there already."

Pepper shrank away from Dalton's outstretched hand. "Yeah, got in an hour or so ago. I'm gonna go check the roof out before the rain really hits hard. Looks like I'll be staying here a few days until the sleet and rain clears."

Nick cleared his throat. "Yeah, um, sorry about that, man. I guess this wasn't the weekend to head up there."

Dalton lowered to the ground and leaned his head on the hard, dusty floor. "Come here, boy."

"What's that?"

"Oh, nothing. I brought Pepper up here with me and the phone frightened him. Don't worry about the weather. It'll be fine. I'll get some things done inside. There's plenty to do."

"Well, remember how you were going to be eating with us tonight and Susan invited her sister over to meet you?"

Dalton abandoned his best mate under the couch to let him relax a bit, stood and adjusted the belt on his hips. "Yeah, I remember. Your wife's one persistent lady."

"I know, and you're not the only one that resorted to running away on Christmas Eve to escape the blind date," Nick said in a rush, making Dalton think he wanted to plow through his next words before Dalton had a chance to process them.

Dalton leaned against the counter and pulled the phone cord clear. "I didn't run away."

"Sure, man. You keep telling yourself that. Anyway, her sister apparently didn't like the setup either, so she bolted."

A slight scratching at Dalton's pride made the girl a little more intriguing. "I guess I can't blame her. Maybe sometime in the future we can meet when we both are more up for it."

"Don't worry about it. I'm pretty sure Sara will bolt every time. So you're off the hook."

Crunching gravel caught his attention and he

leaned toward the window to see headlights blinking between the trees. A car bounced along the rough terrain. "You expecting someone at the cabin? Looks like there's a car headed my way."

"Yeah, well. As I was saying Sara didn't want to meet you."

Dalton cringed at the nail of rejection driving hard into his ego. The nail left by his ex-wife that repeatedly dug into his psyche, reminding him he was half a man. "You said that already." Perhaps all the amazing things Nick had told him about his wife's sister were true and he should've given it a shot sooner. Of course, no one was that perfect for him. Especially a beautiful, smart divorcee that didn't want any more kids. The pain of his divorce, his loss of his child, his loss of all possibility of family pounded deep into his soul.

"Well, her chosen refuge was their cabin, hiding out under the pretense of clearing some stuff out. Apparently, she wanted to make sure she put some distance, weather, and anything else she could between her and tonight's dinner."

Dalton ran a hand through his disheveled hair, reminding him he still hadn't gotten that haircut. "Um, dude. I'm at the cabin."

"Yeah, I know." Nick sighed. "That's why I'm warning you." Nick's tone took a turn toward exacerbation as if Dalton wasn't catching on quick enough.

He heard a scraping sound and leaned into the window, pressing his head to the cool glass. The silver car had slid a few feet, coming too close to the embankment, but the wheel caught traction again and

Nick's sister-in-law she managed to maneuver further up the drive. The roads wouldn't allow either of them to leave the cabin at this point. "If she didn't want to meet me then why'd she drive all the way up here?" He dropped his head to his hands. "No. Don't tell me."

Nick cleared his throat. "Yep, you got it. She doesn't know you're there. Good luck." The phone went dead before Dalton could get another word out.

Pepper crawled to the edge of the sofa and poked his wet, black nose out.

"You know that friend of mine? He's a coward. Bite him next time you see him."

Pepper whined his disapproval.

Dalton took a long breath of musty old cabin smell and opened the front door. So much for a quiet, relaxing weekend in an out-of-the-way cabin where he wouldn't have to see anyone. Instead, he was about to step into an awkward situation of epic proportions.

The bitter wind hit his face with an icy lashing. The woman, Sara, dressed in a thick coat, hood over her head wrangled with something in her back seat. His feet crunched against the snow as he rounded the car. After clearing his throat several times, he tried a greeting. "Hello."

No response.

Sara back-stepped, bags in hand, shut the door and turned. Her eyes, the bluest blue on the planet, widened. Her lips parted and a silent scream, more of a blast of rushed breath, escaped. Her feet slid and she flew backwards, feet overhead, and landed with a loud smack against the ice. The contents of the two bags spread across the rocky drive.

"Are you okay?" Dalton crouched by her side.

She grabbed the back of her head with one hand and kicked her feet at him. "Get away from me." Her screech echoed through the woods, followed by Pepper's barking. Chunks of ice cracked and spread beneath her high-heeled, sexy shoes. She grabbed her purse, her hand fishing for something inside. "Who are you? What are you doing here? If you come near me, I'll blow you—"

Dalton sidestepped with his hands up. "Wait, you don't understand. I'm Dalton, I was sent here by Nick to work on the cabin. He didn't know you'd be here."

She kept her grip on something inside her bag, not bothering to pull free of the twisted straps around her arm. "You know Nick?"

Dalton lowered his hands to his side. "Yes."

Sara looked up, those crystal blue eyes narrowing at him. "What's his wife's name?"

"Susan."

"Susan didn't tell me you'd be here."

"She didn't know."

Sara relinquished whatever weapon resided in her purse and shook her head. "This isn't good."

Dalton scooted closer with a cautious step. "We better get you inside before you freeze to death."

She tucked her legs under her knees. "I can't believe this. All I wanted was a quiet weekend away from another lame blind date. A weekend alone," Sara mumbled, but Dalton caught her meaning loud and clear.

So she'd already formed an opinion of him, but hadn't he done the same? He pictured some desperate loser who couldn't get a date and resorted to having her sister set her up with any friend of Nick's she could find. Why else would a sister set her up with someone who failed at his first marriage?

"Here. Let me help you." Dalton took her by the arm, but her feet kept sliding against the slushy pavement. He wrapped his arms around her waist to keep her standing. She was a little thing, only reaching his shoulders, and she fit easily in his embrace. He wanted her to lift her head, to see those eyes up close, but all he saw was the hood covering her head.

"I can—" She pushed from his arms only to fall to her knees once more. "Ouch!"

"Um, as sexy as those heels are, they're not going to work for walking around here on the ice."

Sara giggled. A sweet, yeah-I-got-that-part kind of laugh. "Yeah, I thought I'd change out of my work clothes when I got here. I guess I miscalculated the weather a little."

Dalton reached under her and scooped her up in his arms. "I think it's best I carry you in for now. If you keep flailing about, you're going to end up seriously hurt and there's no way an ambulance is going to make it up here tonight."

She froze in his arms, as if the wind had whipped through her body petrifying her in an instant. He held her closer to his chest and her body relaxed a little against him.

"Wait. My stuff." Sara squirmed in his arms.

"I'll come back for it. For now, let's get you out of these wet clothes and by a fire."

She stiffened once more.

"No, that's not...I mean—"

Sara giggled again, the sound doing something strange to his chest. The sound of laughter was something he hadn't heard from his ex-wife in years. "I got your meaning. No worries."

He climbed the steps and kicked open the door. Pepper sat only a few feet inside, but disappeared under the couch the moment they crossed the threshold.

"I think you can put me down now," Sara said.

"Oh, right." He lowered her to her feet with ease.

She kicked her sexy heels to the side and lowered to her knees. "He's adorable." She leaned down and extended her hand to Pepper. Pepper edged a little closer and nudged Sara's pale hand, licking the pink polish at the tips of her fingers.

"I think he likes you. Pepper never says *hello* to strangers. He's shy and skittish most of the time."

Pepper scooted a little further out from under the couch and rested his head near her leg. "He doesn't look so shy right now," she said, her face split into a smile.

"No, he doesn't." Dalton chuckled. *Crazy mutt.*

He could see a shiver rake through her small frame. She had to be chilled to the bone from falling in the slush with such thin clothing on, not to mention her bare legs. Legs that extended longer than he would have expected, considering her petite build. "Take your damp coat off."

She turned her head and a teasing smile quirked at the side of her lips. "I'm not that kind of girl."

"I didn't—"

"Relax. You just startled me outside. If you're a friend of Nick's and managed to receive the stamp of approval from my little sis, I'm sure you're cool." She stood and unzipped her oversized coat. It slid down her thin frame, revealing more of an hourglass shape than he'd expected. The long skirt and fitted bright red top accentuated her curves. He swallowed. A loud swallow. Pepper moaned, as if to say *snap-out-of-it. You're being pathetic, dude.*

Dalton grabbed the old afghan from the back of the couch and wrapped it around her shoulders. His fingers grazed the exposed part of her neck, causing a static spark between them. The electricity revved through his body, as if awakening him for the first time since he discovered he would never be able to have a child. He shook off the sadness and inept feelings. "I'll be right back. After I get your stuff, I'll start a fire."

Dalton bolted from the room, away from the beautiful woman, from the shock of her porcelain skin, from the mesmerizing gaze of those endless depths of blue, and most of all, from the thought that he could be a real man once again.

CHAPTER THREE

Sara eyed the wood-walled cabin with iron doorknobs, large brick hearth, and worn floorboards. She'd expected a panic attack by the influx of memories, but nothing had invaded her consciousness. Yet. Well, except for the man with broad shoulders, a deep, sexy voice, and dark, I-just-got-out-of-bed hair. His entire look was animalistic and raw. Nothing like Jack with his metrosexual style, and perfect hair that took longer to style than hers.

Dalton's strength surprised her when he'd lifted her with ease from the ground. Yet, his soft touch made her think he was the product of some sort of crazy experiment in manly perfection. He had to be a loser, with a girlfriend in every city, or married, or gay, or all of the above. But the biggest question was, what was he doing here *today*?

With a shake of her head, she tossed some logs onto the grate in the large fireplace. She retrieved a newspaper from the hearth and glanced at the date stamped on the front. *December 24, 1992.* All the emotions she'd expected when she walked into the living room bombarded her in a rush. Her lungs seized.

Her breath fought for release, but she couldn't get her lungs to obey her commands. A full-on panic attack threatened.

A car door slammed and she willed herself not to lose it not now, not in front of him. She didn't cry, not in front of anyone. Especially not in front of a stranger, a hot stranger that would no doubt report to Nick about her mental break, who would eventually tell her over-intrusive little sister. She crumbled the newspaper and shoved it under the logs then struck a match and set the haunting memories aflame.

The paper shrunk into charred pebbles, and the wood slowly caught fire. Her breathing eased and her heart slowed. Crackles sounded and Pepper edged out from under the sofa. With his head hung low, he army-crawled to her side. The poor submissive dog shivered, so she sat on the floor by the fire and patted her thigh to invite him closer. He eased to her side and rested his head in her lap, as if to comfort her instead of the opposite. Perhaps that was what she needed, a dog. It had to be better than a man. Maybe Susan was right, she shouldn't get back together with Jack. How could she not try, though, for Josh's sake.

The door flew open. Dalton slung grocery bags around, balancing her duffle and purse on his shoulder and her briefcase in the crook of his arm. He kicked the door shut with his foot. "I think I got it all. Although, that isn't much food."

She shrugged. "I don't eat much."

"Well, I do. Good thing I'm a great cook and brought plenty of supplies."

He can cook? Jack believed cooking was women's

work.

Dalton placed her duffle, briefcase, and purse by her side with an inquisitive quirk of an eyebrow. "Hey, you started a fire already?"

"Yeah. Why? You think a girl can't build a fire?" *Stop being combative.* Susan's voice rang in her head.

"No, I know a girl can start a fire. My sister was a Girl Scout. She could beat me at fire-building on every camping trip we took growing up. I was just envious you started it so quick. It would've taken me at least ten minutes." He gave her a charming smile. "I'm glad you're here. Now I won't have to worry about freezing to death."

He's glad I'm here? He didn't want to tell her the proper way to build a fire, or point out each mistake she'd made? "Okay, I'll make a deal with you. You don't judge me for my lack of cooking skills and I won't judge you for your lack of fire-building skills."

"Deal." Dalton held out a strong hand that nearly devoured hers in size, and she shook it. A gentle, yet strong grasp told her he possessed confidence but also sensitivity. She'd shaken a lot of hands at the university when interviewing perspective students and felt confident in her ability to judge a person based on the simple gesture.

She couldn't help but wonder about this man, with his strong body and handsome face. What other family did he have besides a sister? The dust in the air flittered through the muted light from the single table lamp, compounding the awkward silence. What else had Susan told her about Dalton and his family? For once, she wished she'd listened to her. Sara struggled not to look at his left hand, but her gaze traveled there anyway.

He splayed his fingers. "No ring."

Busted. Heat flooded her cheeks faster than the fire engulfing the wood in the hearth. "Um...I..."

"You? Your divorce is final, right? I should ask before we sleep together—I mean, sleep in this cabin together. I wouldn't want your husband busting down the door and coming after me with an axe."

The thought of Jack wielding an axe in a custom suit and manicured nails made her laugh. He probably couldn't even lift an axe. The man was all *metro this* and *urban that*. Total city boy who thought Pilates and yoga were tough workouts. Not that there was anything wrong with a man doing Pilates, but when he spent all *her* money and his time at the studio instead of working there was an issue. For years, she told herself there were worse things, that he could have been an alcoholic or a druggy, but it didn't change the fact he used her then threw her away when he'd found a new sugar momma. "No husband. Not anymore."

Pepper lifted his head and licked her arm.

"Hey, stop that," Dalton scolded.

"It's fine. Most love I've had in a while." *Seriously, Sara? How pathetic.* This guy must think she was a total loser. She patted Pepper on the head and grabbed her duffle. "I guess I'll go change into something less damp."

"I'm divorced, too. I guess we have that in common." Dalton grabbed the poker and jabbed at the pieces of wood in the fireplace. "You know, Sara, I tend to shy away from the divorce comment, too, but I think

I finally realized something. It's not a blemish on our love record, but a note that we're schooled in the hardships of marriage. That makes us head of the class and working on more of a master's degree."

That was a strange analogy. Did he know she worked at a university? Of course he did. Susan had probably told him everything about her, like she'd told her everything about him. Well, all the good stuff anyway. "It's funny. I know so much about you, but Susan never told me your last name."

He placed the poker back in the rack and faced her with a serious look on his clean-shaven face. Only a small scar above his right eyebrow showed any flaws to his perfection. Then he smiled. "It's Scott. I'm Dalton Scott. It's nice to meet you."

She eyed his devious smile, as if he knew something she didn't. "Wait. How did Susan know I'd be up here? She's resorted to a new low this time. And you—"

"No, I didn't know that you'd be here. Trust me." Dalton waved his hands. "I didn't know until you drove up the driveway. I was on the phone with Nick the Coward. He called to tell me you were on your way. That you didn't know that I was here. Apparently, Nick never told his wife I was ditching dinner. I bet he was hoping once you showed she couldn't go ballistic on him in front of you."

He'd abandoned the blind date, too. "That wasn't nice of you to stand me up, you know."

Dalton crossed his arms over his broad chest and stared her down. "You did the same thing. At least I told Nick I wouldn't be going."

"Okay, I guess you have a point." Sara smiled, a mischievous, playful feeling invigorating her. She sashayed over to him and captured his gaze. "Your loss anyway."

His kissable lips parted, but before he could say another word, she headed for the bedroom and shut the door behind her. What had gotten into her? Did she just flirt? She hadn't flirted since...before Jack. What was she doing? Susan must have gotten into her head when she'd coached her for Christmas Eve dinner, telling her to remain light and playful. Fun and alluring instead of like the gloomy man repellant she usually was. Something she'd perfected over the last year.

Analyzing the baggy sweatshirt and mom jeans she brought with her, she sighed. If anything was man repellant, those jeans were. Not that she wanted to impress the man, or have anything to do with him beyond this epic fail of a weekend, but she couldn't send him away with the memory of the frumpy girl. Instead of dressing in her day clothes, she pulled on her thermal leggings and a tank top. Eyeing his clothes in the corner hanging over the chair, she noticed a flannel button up shirt. It had to be better than the oversized sweatshirt. She snatched it from the chair and took a deep inhale of the earthy, sexy aroma. Something stirred inside her. Wow, the scent was enough to send a woman into heat. She slid her arms into the soft fabric and wrapped it around her, loving the feel of a sportsman's shirt. Not the Egyptian cotton and satiny fabric that Jack liked so much.

Pots and pans clanked in the kitchen and the aroma of coffee seeped under the door. The thought of

Dalton cooking, in his hip-hugging jeans and crooked come-hither smile, sent her heart into a cadence of expectation. She opened the door and forced her chin high. "I borrowed your shirt. I hope you don't mind. I didn't know anyone would be here, so I didn't bring much."

The throaty sound that came from Dalton made her feel noticed. His eyes, raking over her, made her feel attractive. And the way his eggs were burning made her feel like the most important thing in the room.

"Oh, shoot." He grabbed the skillet and moved it off the burner.

This man was different in every way—attentive, helpful, attractive, funny, strong, and most of all, nothing like Jack. Susan hadn't lied about any of it. Fur slid beneath her hand and Pepper leaned into her. "Is he from the shelter you volunteer at?"

Dalton dumped the eggs into the sink and cracked a few more. "Yes, he's a little damaged, but a good friend."

"Aren't we all? I think he's perfect." Sara watched the man in front of her moving about the kitchen with purpose and ease. Susan had raved about his cooking, his job as a fireman and contractor, his work at the shelter. Somehow, the snapshot hadn't translated into the man in front of her. The words had lacked the detail of the emotional intensity in his eyes, the set of his strong jaw. What else had her sister's words not captured?

Dalton cracked two more eggs into the pan, which spluttered and popped, filling the room with the aroma of breakfast and home.

"Honestly, he doesn't usually let strangers pet him. I've never seen him take to someone like he has to you. Most of all, I can't believe he's come out from under the couch."

Sara rubbed behind his ears and Pepper leaned into her leg with all his weight. "I guess he has good taste." She held her breath for a moment, but she couldn't hold her tongue. She had to know. "Did he not take to your ex-wife?"

His hands froze, but the eggs continued to bubble and the sausage sizzled. "She's never met Pepper. She wasn't a dog person. I rescued him after we were divorced."

For some reason the fact that Pepper hadn't connected with his ex-wife made her happy. This unknown woman had to be a model, professional cheerleader, or Donald Trump rich. Something to catch this man's eye. Men like him didn't go after plain-Janes and the collegiate type. Did he?

"What about you? Have any pets?" Dalton plated the food and poured coffee into two mismatched mugs. The rich aroma heated her insides in anticipation.

"No. My ex was allergic. Actually, he's allergic to everything."

"Everything?" Dalton's eyebrow rose.

"According to my sister, yes."

"Ah, yes. My sister had her own words for my ex, too. Family tends to obliterate the exes, don't they? Let me guess, he's allergic to being faithful, or work, or being a good husband."

"According to my sister? All of the above." Sara took her plate and cup and found a spot on the floor near the fire. "I still can't believe we both ended up here."

"Do you mind it so much? If you want to be alone, you can take the bedroom and I'll hang out here quietly until the roads clear."

Sara forked a piece of sausage. "I'm surprised I'm saying this, but no. I like your company. I mean, all I wanted on my way up here was to escape my sister's meddling and having to put on an act that my heart wanted nothing to do with."

Dalton chewed some eggs then took a sip of his coffee. "Me, too. I'm not ready for a show and the grandstanding that comes with a blind date. That awkward moment where you're both being polite, but you're uncomfortably aware you're under a microscope. Knowing that your every move will be overanalyzed once you leave."

"Yep, you know my sister."

Dalton took a napkin and dotted it to her chin, his body invading her space, a welcome invasion.

"You've got a speck of dirt left on your chin from when you fell." His hand returned to his lap, but he remained close, his gaze traveling over her face. "You know, I'm glad we met here and not at your sister's house."

Sara rubbed her chin, feeling like there was a pigpen of dirt on her face. "You are?"

"Yeah, I don't know your sister that well, but I know mine. We would've never had a chance to relax and just hang out. It would be all questions, nudging, and innuendos. I could shut my own sister down, but I wouldn't cross Susan. I think Nick is a little scared of her."

"A little? Trust me, you would be, too. The woman doesn't take *no* for an answer. I think you're right. It's better we met here."

Dalton leaned back against the sofa and smiled, a mischievous bad boy smile. "Let's make a deal and skip all the awkward moments and pretentious ways of a blind date and just be ourselves."

Sara studied him. For some insane reason, she thought it was a good idea. It was twenty-four, forty-eight hours tops. Who cared if he knew the real, pathetic divorcee with a kid and a stealing ex-husband. *Says the woman who abandoned her mommy jeans.* "Okay, so we can be open and honest and not be someone we're not?"

"That's right. So, tell me, should I be scared of you, like Nick is of Susan? Don't get me wrong. I don't mind a feisty woman. I'm just curious."

Sara couldn't help but laugh. She and Susan couldn't be more different. "No. I'm a boring college professor. My sister's an attorney."

"I bet she's good at her job." Dalton scooped his remaining eggs up and devoured them.

She took a few bites and savored the salty goodness. "She is. Since we were little girls she could argue both sides of a debate until you didn't know what you were supposed to be arguing about anymore."

"But you became a Mrs. Smarty-pants, too. You gotta be smart to be a college professor."

"Adjunct professor."

"Hey, from a guy who has a bachelor's in history, you're definitely a smarty-pants." He retrieved their plates before she could stand.

"Okay. We're supposed to be ourselves, right?"

"Yes, ma'am." Dalton washed the plates and stacked them on a drying rack.

"Are you doing dishes to impress me, or do you normally do women's work."

"Hey, be careful what you say. We firefighters have to do all our own cooking and cleaning. And don't let Bear hear you call it women's work."

"Bear?" Sara tossed another log on the fire and he joined her on the rug in front of it to warm their hands.

"Yeah, he's two hundred and fifty pounds of solid muscle and attitude. He also does dishes in his grandmother's apron. It's pink with ruffles and no one would dare tell him it makes him look like a sissy."

Sara pictured this guy in her head and nearly fell over laughing. "I'd like to see that someday."

"Sounds like a plan." Dalton's eyes darted to the floor and she swore his cheeks weren't just red from the reflection of the fire.

"I'd like that." A draft blew under the front door, chilling her. She wished she'd brought the quilt back from the bedroom after she'd changed to stave the cold from her body. The cabin was old and rundown, mimicking the way she'd felt in the last few months. "Are you close with your family?"

Dalton sat cross-legged and patted his thigh for Pepper to rest his head on. The dog snuggled up to him. "We do all the holidays together when my schedule allows, and we talk on the phone every Sunday, so as much as most families are. My mother still says she's shocked that my sister and I didn't kill each other growing up. I used to get so mad when she'd best me at something until I saw her deck a boy who tried to put the moves on her. When I saw the guy fly over the back of his chair, I became one proud brother."

"Good for her." Sara took a whiff of the manly aroma of his shirt around her body.

"Were you close with your sister when you were growing up?" Dalton asked.

She nodded, but didn't know what else to say. How could she tell him that when you lose both your parents within three years of each other, at such a young age, you tend to cling to the only family you have left?

The fire crackled, the familiar sound taking her back to that long ago Christmas Eve. She'd held tight to her sister while her mother screamed at her father. Susan had wailed in her lap, scared by all the noise of their parents fighting and doors slamming.

"Where did you go?" Dalton quirked his head to one side, a fluff of hair falling over his forehead.

Sara closed her eyes and steadied her emotions. Even Jack didn't know about that night. She never spoke about it. Not to her aunt, not to Susan. No one. "It's nothing."

"Remember, we're being ourselves. If you don't want to tell me, it's fine. I don't mean to dig where I don't belong, but you had that look when I came in with your stuff. Like you were reliving something."

"I was," Sara whispered.

His hand covered her trembling fingers and she thought for a moment she could actually share such a deep secret with a stranger. A stranger that she knew everything about, but didn't know him at all.

"Remember no microscope, no innuendos, no pushing us together."

"You're right." She took a deep breath. "I was lost in a memory." She tried to swallow past the dryness in her throat. "I was remembering the night my father left. It was here, in this cabin on Christmas Eve when I was five years old." She cleared her throat and pulled her hand away. "It was a long time ago. No need to talk about it now." She rose to her knees and went for the poker on the hearth, but he snagged her hand.

The fire crackled and Pepper snuggled to her side, helping to calm her rollercoaster emotions.

Dalton edged closer. He tipped her head to force her to look at him. "And no judgment."

Sara trembled, the words stuck halfway to her lips. "He died. Slid off the bridge. He abandoned my mother, my sister, and me that night, and never returned."

CHAPTER FOUR

Dalton wanted to pull Sara into his arms and hold her. The way her eyes strained against the sadness, yet didn't shed a tear, snapped his heart in a trap. After five years of Nicole's hysterics and using emotion to get what she wanted, he thought he'd never feel for a woman again. He was wrong. He stroked her pale, soft cheek with his thumb and she sucked in a quick breath. "I'm so sorry for what you've been through."

Sara searched the cabin, as if looking for answers and he knew that was what she came up here to find. She drifted away from his touch and at that moment, he knew he'd do anything to make her pain go away.

He straightened, ignoring the twinge of sadness at her pulling away from him. Following her gaze, he said, "This place needs something."

Sara shrugged and looked around the room again. "Well, new walls and a new roof to start."

"I agree, but I'm not climbing that roof tonight. I'll leave that for Santa. What do you say to cutting down a small tree?"

Sara rewarded his plan with a smile. "You have any popcorn?"

"Popcorn?"

She stood up and offered her hand to him with a determined set to her brow. "Yeah, you can't have a Christmas tree if you don't decorate it. Then it's just a tree."

Dalton took her tiny hand in his and pushed from the ground. She held tight, her strength surprised him. "You have any boots? If not, you'll have to trust me to pick the tree."

"I am a professor, you know." She winked, her long lashes playfully drawing his attention. He released her hand so she could retrieve her shoes.

Pepper bounced out of the room at her heels. They always said dogs were good judges of character. The only time Nicole had come over after the divorce, Pepper had growled and barked. Yep, good judge of character.

The warmth in the room faded with her absence. He rubbed his arms as if he'd lost his coat. Strange, this cabin was drafty and old, but warm and cozy all at the same time. He hoped to cheer her up and keep her from those haunting memories that seemed to keep sweeping her soul. For the first time in months, he had a desire to help a human instead of an animal. Of course, animals were easy and faithful. There was no fear of lying or manipulation. Was Sara truly all Nick had made her out to be? Could Pepper see something beyond what a human could detect?

He shoved each of his feet into his boots and bent to lace them. Pepper trotted out and sat at the front door. "You wanna go outside?"

Woof.

Dalton scratched his head and eyed the dog that had done nothing but mope and cower since he'd adopted him. Now he sat on his haunches, wagging his tail with that I'm-excited dog face.

"I think he does." Sara snagged her coat and slid her arms inside, covering her curves once more. He watched her graceful movements, like that of a dancer. "He wants to pick out a Christmas tree with us."

"I think you're right." Dalton buttoned his coat and opened the front door. Pepper darted outside, but his paws couldn't get traction on the ice and he kept sliding.

"Careful, boy. You're gonna get hurt." Sara raced after him, sliding on the ice. Dalton grabbed her hand, thankful for an excuse to hold it once more even if their skin was blocked by their gloves.

"We best not go too far." He scanned the sloping front yard full of damp earth, downed trees, and scattered sprigs of pine. Beyond the first line of trees, he spotted one stubby one that reached about four feet tall. It wasn't fat, but it would hold a few strings of popcorn and whatever else they could find.

The cold beat at the edges of his coat, as if attempting to find an entrance to steal the warmth from his body. He snugged her hat further down over her head and tucked her hair inside. "Need to stay warm out here. I don't want you catching a cold on my watch."

"I thought you were a fireman not a doctor," She smiled, her straight white teeth and full lips promising an amazing kiss, though he doubted he'd ever get to test the theory. He averted his gaze before he lost all sense.

She squeezed his hand and pointed to a tree stump near her car. "Guess we should grab that on the way."

He followed her finger to see an ax impaled into the heart of it. "You sure you're not the fireman?"

Pepper barked, sliding left and right next to them.

"Me? No. You're the one who's going to wield that thing. I don't even think I can lift it."

"Ha. I don't know. I have a feeling you could beat me at a lumberjack competition any day, but I appreciate you sparing my male ego."

She shrugged, her oversized coat poofing out at her ears making her look like an adorable navy blue snowwoman.

They traversed the icy ground with care, clinging to one another, the sides of the cars, trees, rocks, and anything else they could to make it to the other side of the drive. His inner firefighter cursed him the entire way, screaming that they should remain inside before one of them ended up with a concussion, but he'd do anything to see this woman happy. He had a feeling she hadn't had one good Christmas since she was a little girl. And he'd admit, at least to himself, that he needed this just as much as she. He hadn't been able to even hear the words *Merry Christmas* without cringing.

"Now *you* look lost." Sara reached for the axe and tugged, but it didn't budge.

He tried to hide his anguish and concentrated on extracting the axe from the stump. One good yank and he slung it over his shoulder. Pepper peed on a nearby tree then slid to a stop in front of them, shivering.

"Oh, he's cold." Sara peered out from under her hooded coat and hat next to him. "We better get that tree and get back inside before he freezes. But don't think I'm letting you out of telling me what that look was about just now. This is an honest place, remember?"

He nodded, his mind racing with what to say. How could he say the words aloud when he couldn't even think them.

With cautious steps, they made their way over to the chosen tree and with only three chops, the tree gave and fell to the ground. "It's small, but I think it'll work."

"It's a Charlie Brown tree. It's like the one I had the first year it was just my son and me alone at Christmas. He'd fall asleep under the low branches, as if he were in the woods. He's always liked the outdoors," she said, her voice fading.

"Do you ever take him camping?"

"I know nothing about camping, fishing, or football...although, I started reading *Football For Dummies* when Jack left. I figured I had to play both mother and father if Josh had any chance of being okay with a single mom."

Dalton snagged the thick end of the trunk, while Sara took the top. "Good thing you know a fireman that's not only handy, but a good outdoorsman."

Sara did that playful-grin thing that had nearly done him in earlier. It was even more endearing with her puffy hood framing her delicate face. His knees shook, as if he'd hiked several miles through the slush to get to the cabin. If he didn't know better, he'd swear her smile could bring him to his knees.

White flakes drifted in the air around them, quickly becoming a swarm. Dots of white sprinkled Sara's dark coat. She clung to a tree trunk as she maneuvered up the last slope. "Hey, we might get a white Christmas after all. It would sure be nicer than this slush."

"We probably will. I have a feeling this Christmas is gonna be a little brighter than we'd thought." He watched her, waiting for her body to stiffen, but he couldn't tell under the big coat.

She paused at the front door, balancing the tree while she opened the door. "I think you're right."

The fire draped the inside of the cabin with a warm glow. "Let's set it down here. I'll make a stand for it."

They lowered the tree to the old worn wood floor. He unlaced and removed his boots, but Sara's hands were beet red and she fumbled with her laces.

"Here. Let me help." He unlaced her boots and pulled them off, then cupped her hands in his. "You need some better gloves." The redness of her hands concerned him. He blew warm air onto her skin. To his relief, she didn't stiffen or pull away. Instead, she closed her eyes and leaned into him.

"Come here. Those socks don't look too thick either." He led her over to the fireplace where Pepper had already claimed his warm spot. "Sit."

She slid out of her coat and tossed it to the side, flecks of snow scattering over the floor. "Oops. I hope there's still a mop here."

"Don't worry about it. We'll get it cleaned up. Right now I'm worried about getting you warm again." He snagged the afghan from the bedroom and wrapped it around her shoulders, then removed his own coat and stoked the fire before he returned to her side. "Let me have your foot. I want to get your circulation moving."

"Are all firemen this attentive?" Sara teased, but placed a thin, pink-socked foot on his lap.

As he rubbed her toes and foot back to life, she leaned her head back and closed her eyes. His attention was rewarded with a small moan. A moan that made him smile.

"Yep, much better way to spend Christmas than moping up here by myself. Of course, I've never been much for wallowing. I find it to be a waste of time."

"It must've been tough. I don't know what it's like to lose a parent, but I definitely know what it's like to lose someone you love." He set her foot to the side and took her other one. Once more, she rewarded him with a moan of delight.

The scent of pine filled the room, the fire warmed his side, and Pepper barked his own happiness. Yep, not a bad Christmas Eve after all.

"You've lost someone? Is that what you were thinking about outside?"

He forced his hands to continue moving, to keep filling his lungs and releasing his breath. The way he'd had to concentrate on Christmas Eve last year. A short nod was all he could manage beyond the repetitive movement of his hands.

Sara slid her foot from his lap and rose to her knees. Her hand cupped his cheek. "It was someone close to you. I can see that. Remember, no judgment. No expectations. No overanalyzing everything. If you don't want to tell me, don't. If you want to, then I'm here to listen."

He cleared his throat. "My son. He died at birth. On Christmas Eve last year."

CHAPTER FIVE

The slack of Dalton's lips, the wide eyes, and deep sorrow filling his gaze nearly chopped her heart in two. His eyes moistened with unshed tears. She knew this man was strong. Based on the information Susan had told her, this man was a rock. A person who would throw himself into harm's way to save another. But here, now, he was vulnerable.

She swallowed the lump in her throat and caressed his cheek, allowing him a moment to feel her touch, before she tipped his head to her shoulder and stroked his soft hair. They remained there, together, embracing one another for a long moment. It was strange, but she felt closer to him than she ever had during the years she was married to Jack. He was the stranger, not the man here. This man she understood. They connected through their shared grief, but was there more between them than just a touch of healing?

The fire crackled and he lifted his head, as if to check to make sure it was under control. He swiped his eyes. "I-I..."

She touched his shoulder. "No judgment." This kind of emotion had to be difficult for a man like him.

Especially in front of someone else, something she understood. She longed to be closer to him, to hold him, to make his pain go away.

They sat gazing at each other, as if communicating without words. She slid her hand to his neck and pressed her lips to his cheek. His scent overwhelmed her and she thought she'd fall into him, but his arms wrapped around her. She remained on her knees, his face snuggling into her neck, their bodies pressed together. The warmth seeped into her soul.

"I think we both came up here to wallow in our own pain, but ended up finding each other. Perhaps we were meant to help each other through this Christmas," he whispered.

With Dalton's arms wrapped around her body, his deep voice and warmth comforting her, something told her she was exactly where she was meant to be. "Perhaps fate knows better than we do." She chuckled at the words from her past.

"What?" He leaned back and tucked her hair gently behind her ear, his lips only inches from her own.

"That's what my father used to say. I remember it because whenever I'd pitch a fit over something, he'd always say that. The night he left, he whispered that to me."

"What do you think he meant?" Dalton asked.

She shook her head. "I've thought about that often. I don't know if it's the little girl in me hoping he meant something more than just to abandon us, or if there was something more going on that night. It's always plagued me. I think that's why I came up here."

"I understand. I brought something with me, too." He released her and disappeared into the bedroom, returning a moment later with two small blue socks in his hand. "I had these in my hand when the nurse told me my son didn't make it." His head hung low, shoulders slumped, as if he'd willingly fade into dust to be next to his child once more.

Sara moved to his side and covered his hands with hers. "I'm so sorry. I wish I could make your pain go away."

He half-chuckled, half-cried. "The ironic thing is that the baby wasn't even mine." His hands trembled in hers, his jaw twitched with an angry snap. "I was so excited when I found out my ex, Nicole, was pregnant. I did everything I could to make it work between us, but there was something wrong. I knew it from the first moment she told me, but I ignored it. I kept the nagging feeling at bay and I convinced myself the doctors were wrong. That I could father a child. Or it was a miracle and I had a son of my own. I'd sit there each night rubbing her belly, never wanting to move my hand because I might miss a kick or a thump." He inhaled a stuttered breath.

She squeezed his hands, allowing him to say anything and everything he needed to say. To have someone that would listen and understand.

"It wasn't until the day Nicole lost the baby that she told me I was a fool. That the only reason she stayed was because the baby needed a father, but I wasn't the real dad."

Sara had to concentrate not to squeeze his hands so tight that he'd know the anger that surged through her. This wasn't about her feelings, it was about his healing.

Pepper crawled over and sat at his feet.

"That's when things ended between us for good. On Christmas Eve, I lost a son that wasn't mine, and my wife left me because I'm half a man. That was her words anyway." He shrugged.

She couldn't hold her tongue any longer. She tugged his chin until his eyes met hers then said, "You listen to me. I don't know your ex, but you are one hundred percent a man. There's nothing wrong with you. If you think for a second conception makes you a father, you're wrong. My son has a man in his life that behaves more like a sperm donor than a father, that uses him to manipulate money out of me. Trust me when I say, someday you'll be the most amazing dad."

He sniffed and took a long breath. "I know, and I know that my ex only kept me around because she needed someone to take care of her, but I still long to be a father someday. I don't regret my decision to ignore the truth. Even though I suspected the baby wasn't mine, I never cared. The only regret is that I wasn't allowed to hold my son or say goodbye."

Sara threw her arms around his neck and held him tight. No more words needed to be said. She knew exactly what he'd meant. She'd never had a chance to say goodbye to her father. Perhaps that's why she drove to the cabin, for a chance to finally bury the past, so she could be a better mom for her own son.

She caressed his back, rubbing her hands up and down his strong frame. He pressed his lips to the top of her head before leaning his forehead against hers. "What do you say to me making that tree stand?"

She could hear the emotion drowning him and knew he wanted a lifeline. "Do you like hot chocolate?"

He released her, a little-boy smile creasing his lips. "It's my favorite. Can I have marshmallows on top?"

"That depends," she said.

"On what?"

She glanced at the kitchen. "Do you have any marshmallows?"

"Top shelf, next to the refrigerator."

She sauntered over to the kitchen. "Gee, don't make yourself at home or anything," she said teasingly.

"Good thing I did, or we would've starved or frozen to death by now." He slid his feet in his boots, put on his coat and disappeared out the front door.

Sara found the ingredients, along with popcorn kernels, then heated milk for hot cocoa. Pouring a bit of oil into a saucepan, she dumped popcorn kernels into the pot and covered it with a lid. A hammer sound echoed from outside. For the first time since driving up the mountain, she didn't feel like the ghost of lost yesterdays was haunting her.

The front door flew open and he snagged the small tree, hammering the trunk to the stand before lifting it up and setting it next to the fireplace. She ran over and shoved the door closed to shut out the damp, cold wind.

He stood back, admiring the tree. It only came to his chest, with sparse branches and a few baby pinecones. "I think that'll work."

"It's perfect." It was a little crooked, and a little droopy, but it still sparked a little Christmas spirit. "A Christmas spark."

"What's that?" Dalton asked as he tended the fire, stoking it until it roared to life once more.

"My father. I remembered something else he used to say. At Christmas when we'd put up our tree, I'd look at it and say it felt like Christmas. He'd tell me it was the Christmas spark. The moment that healed our hearts from anything in the previous year and gave us hope for what was to come."

He stared at her a moment, a gentle expression easing the tension in his face. "I like that." He swaggered over and placed a hand on the wall behind her.

Popcorn tapped at the pan lid almost as fast as her pulse raced. He hovered next to her ear, his lips grazing her earlobe with the lightest touch. A touch she wasn't sure if she'd imagined. "I think this is going to be a good Christmas after all."

CHAPTER SIX

The rest of the day was filled with laughter, good food, warm hugs, and playful banter. Sara was like no other woman he'd ever met. She was strong, independent, yet soft and loving. After decorating the tree and playing cards, which he swore she cheated at, they ate the simple beef stew he threw together for dinner.

Everything Nick had told him was a hundred percent true, but there was more to her than just her job, work ethic, beauty, and kindness. She had something that he'd never experienced before, a kind of safe, knowing connection with him. In only a few hours, he felt comfortable enough to say things to her he hadn't shared with anyone. And even with his moment of weakness, he didn't feel embarrassed or like less of a man. Instead, she made him open his heart. Only for a beat or two, but he hadn't allowed himself to feel anything for so long he wasn't sure he could feel anymore.

Sara lifted the bowls from the floor. Her hips swayed with each step, mesmerizing him. "Wow, you really can cook. I can't believe I ate all that." She rubbed her belly, as if stroking his ego once more. "I think the tree looks pretty good with the popcorn on it, but I think I have some decorations we can add somewhere. You mind helping me look?"

"Sure. Where do you think they'll be?"

She tapped her chin, accidentally depositing some soapsuds.

He rounded the corner and wiped them away with his thumb, enjoying the feel of her soft, creamy skin.

She chuckled softly. "Um...thanks. I-I think there are some boxes in the hall and bedroom closets."

He liked the way she responded to his touch. The fire in her eyes and the excitement in her voice made him feel wanted, desired. Something he'd lost over the past year. How he'd gone from college football stud to insecure divorcee he wasn't sure, but he wanted to discover some middle ground. "I'll go look."

Pepper remained by Sara's side while he searched the hall closet. Old photos, toys, and personal items from her childhood filled boxes, stacked and forgotten. He found a small ornate frame with an image of a small child holding a baby. *That's Sara*, he thought. Those eyes were undeniable. He wasn't sure if she'd like the old memories or if it would cause her more sadness, so he put the picture back and closed the closet, figuring she'd go looking if she wanted to relive anything.

He moved to the bedroom and discovered some broken glass ornaments tucked in the corner of the closet, a string of lights that didn't work, and a box marked *Christmas*. He opened the Christmas box to find letters addressed to Sara. They were unopened and obviously old.

"Did you find anything?" Sara entered and she froze, her smile fading instantly.

He clutched a yellowed envelope, wishing he could shove it back in the box, but it was too late. The room remained silent for a long moment, the only sound the occasional howl from a distant coyote. "I found these in this box. They're unopened."

"That's my dad's handwriting." She shuffled closer and dropped to her knees, her hand outstretched. "It matches some documents I found when I cleared out my aunt's house a few months ago."

Pepper joined them, laying his head on her lap. She took the envelope and stared into the Christmas box where the others remained. "It's addressed to me. Are all of them?"

He fanned through the few remaining envelopes. "No, one is to Susan."

She shook her head, her dark hair brushing across her high pink cheeks. A hint of flowers, the ones he smelled earlier, wafted to him. It had to be her shampoo. "I don't understand. Aunt Lisa had to know about these. Why didn't she tell me?"

She stared at the envelope, as if reading the letter inside through the white shield. "Mother had been sick. A brain tumor. They found it back when I was a little girl. I think a few months after my father died. My aunt raised us. Maybe she didn't know about them."

"Probably. By the looks of this cabin, no one's been here for awhile," he offered, hoping it would soothe the deep lines on her forehead. Lines of fear, confusion, and loss. He knew them well.

Her finger slid under the seal and the flap popped open. Pepper scooted closer and Dalton set the boxes aside, scooped Sara into his lap then leaned against the wall. "We'll read them together."

"Thank you," she whispered, her voice cracking under the stress. She unfolded the letter and he saw a long page of scribbled words. "It's from when I was three."

Her shoulders relaxed a little and she leaned into him. The floral aroma pleased him and he stroked her soft hair as she read.

"*Dear Sara Bear,*" she choked. "I'd forgotten he called me that."

Dalton squeezed her to his chest and rested his chin on the top of her head, eyeing the letter as she read.

"*You are the brightest star in the sky. I can't believe this is our third Christmas together. The last three years have flown by, and I cherish every moment we have together. Christmas has always been my favorite time of year. I don't know if you'll remember when you're older, but you love to put on your galoshes and demand to go pick a tree with me. You choose the 'lonely' tree, telling me we have to take it inside because it's small and lonely in the forest. You've always had the biggest heart and I love you with every ounce of my being.*"

Sara lowered the letter and swiped at her tears. "He loved me. But then why did he leave us?"

"I don't know. Maybe one of the other letters will tell you." He kissed her head, hoping to comfort her, the way she'd comforted him only hours earlier.

She sniffled and continued to read, but this time in silence. "He talks about things I'd forgotten. Christmas Eve and our traditions. Some are things we've done together today. Hot chocolate, stringing popcorn, picking out a tree. Apparently my taste in trees hasn't changed." She chuckled.

He watched snow falling outside the window, the light fading from the sky, and listened to the sounds of the forest. Every few moments she'd share a piece of her childhood, sometimes with a smile, other times with a hollow gaze.

Finally, she folded the letter and slipped it back into the envelope then set it aside to retrieve another. "This one's from when I was only a few months old. He carried me into the forest to find my first Christmas tree. Mother was late. They'd driven up separately, so he sat by the fire holding me. Apparently, I was a colicky baby, but when he lit the Christmas tree, I stopped crying and watched the lights. That's when he first told me about the Christmas spark."

The wind blew against the window, sending a draft through the room. She shivered and he wrapped his arms around her waist, tugging her closer to him. She put the letter back and took another. Her body immediately stiffened and he squeezed her. "This is the Christmas before he died. He mentions Mom expecting another baby and that he's worried about her. He sounds a little sad."

His mind went to the worst. The thing he feared most in the world. "Was there something wrong with the baby?"

"No, with my mom. He thinks maybe it's some sort of pregnancy thing. He didn't want to leave me alone with her because she'd had a few episodes of some sort. He says that everything will be perfect next year though, because I'll have a new little brother or sister and Mom will be feeling better by then." She replaced the letter and grabbed the last one. Her hands shook. "It's from the night he died."

"Do you want to take a break?"

She shook her head, but remained stiff in his arms. He cursed himself for finding the letters, for making her suffer through reading them, but he also knew she needed this. She needed to know what happened that night all those years ago. He only hoped it would give her some sort of closure.

The wind picked up and the loose shingles on the roof rattled overhead. He only hoped the roof would keep them dry. It would be a rough night if it didn't hold up in the winter storm.

She opened the letter, but sat silently. He looked and discovered her eyes were closed.

"Do you want me to read it first?" he offered.

She shook her head and took a long breath. "*Dear Sara Bear, you have been my light during this dark time. I'm writing this because I hope someday we'll be okay. I've got both you and your sister locked in the room with me.*" Her voice cracked and all he could do was sit and hold her as she read.

"*Your mother is having another episode. I've tried to get her to see someone, but she won't. There's nothing left for me to do to help her, but I'd do anything to protect you and your little sister. I love your mother even now, but she's sick and needs help. If she was well, she'd want me to do whatever it took to care for you. I hope someday you can forgive me for calling the police on your mother. There was nothing else I could do. If I try to restrain her, she'll call the police and tell them that I harmed her. It's time. I need to go, but next year we'll be together again, the three of us at the cabin making happy memories. This is a magical place full of love and laughter, and it'll be that way again someday. I love you, Sara Bear."*

She closed the letter and broke down. He held her face to his chest as her body shook. "He didn't know. He thought she was crazy."

The sobs took hold and he fought his own tears. He didn't care that they'd only met hours ago. They'd shared a lifetime of pain with each other. He didn't know how it could happen so quick, but he cared for this woman.

They remained clinging to one another for several minutes. The smell of her hair, the warmth of her body, the softness of her skin, the beauty of her soul filling his heart.

"I-I'm sorry. I never cry."

He tilted her tear-streaked face so he could see her and looked into her eyes. "Don't you dare apologize, Remember, no judgment here, only arms for hugging and ears for listening."

She rewarded his words with an I'm-gonna-be-okay-now smile. "Let's go back to the fire. It's chilly in here."

"You're right. I'll find some more blankets for your bed and grab a few for the couch," he offered, not wanting to release her, but knowing he didn't want to ruin anything they were developing here by going too fast and making her uncomfortable.

She slid from his lap and he offered his hand to help her up. He pulled her into a hug and wiped the tears from her face.

"I must be a fright." She looked away, but he tilted her chin to him.

His desire beat at his restraint until he couldn't hold back any longer. It might have been the pain that still flickered in her eyes, or the way he longed to be closer to her, but he lowered his lips to hers. Only for a brief second, but in that second the world stopped. The snow, the wind, the pain, it all ceased to exist, replaced with only the taste of Sara's lips.

CHAPTER SEVEN

Sara's pulse raced. Her skin seared. Despite what he said, this man had no trouble starting fires. Before she could ground herself in the moment and respond, his lips were gone.

She wanted to pull him back, to kiss him and let him know how she longed to be close to him, but he slipped away. Worse than that, she let him go. Her head felt light with the idea of letting this man near her. Even for a man who had a stamp of approval from her sister, she'd shared too much. She'd shared more with him in a day than she had in years of marriage with her ex-husband. That was the problem. She cared. It had been so long since she cared about anyone besides her son, and even he had been taken away from her this Christmas.

First her father then her mother, her aunt, and even her sister, married and busy with her own family. All she had was her son, who was in New York. Could she do this? Could she allow a man close to her, if he was just going to walk out of her life again in another twenty-four hours? This was a weekend of healing for them both, a safe zone. But then what? He'd get what he needed and be gone, the way her ex had gotten her money then disappeared until he needed more money.

"What are you thinking about?" Dalton's voice broke through the rampage of mixed emotions swirling in her head.

"Um, nothing really." She walked to the window and looked out at the falling snow. The beauty was indescribable. The serenity of it soothed her heart to a slower beat until it finally returned to normal. "How long do you think the weather will last?"

"I'm not sure. I'd say the snow might stop tomorrow, but the roads probably won't be passable until the day after at least. Depends on if it's going to warm up or if they can get any plows up here. Why?" Dalton asked, his words sounding gruff, distant.

She spun around and shook off the worry of what came next, noticing a quilt up on the top shelf of the closet at her side. "No reason. Here. This should be warm enough for you." She took the blanket to the couch and placed it on the armrest. The thought of returning to his side by the fire invited her to sit, but the thought of getting even closer to this man when he'd be gone in a day or two churned her stomach. She yawned and stretched. "I think I'll turn in early. I'm tired after everything that's happened today. Why don't you take the bed and I'll take the couch. I'm much smaller than you. You'd be more comfortable in the bedroom."

"Sorry. Not happening." Dalton fluffed a pillow. "I'll be fine right here. Pepper will keep me company." Pepper trotted off to the bedroom as if on cue, making his stand on his sleeping arrangements. "Traitor."

She shifted between feet. "It's really okay—"

"No, it's not." He scooped her up in his arms as if she weighed less than their little Christmas tree, followed Pepper, and placed her on the bed. He drew the covers up and tucked them under her chin. Pepper jumped on the bed and snuggled up to her side. "I'll remember that later," he said to Pepper. "So much for man's best friend."

She couldn't help but chuckle. He kissed her forehead, as if she were a little girl, and went to the door. He paused, his hand resting on the light switch. "If you need anything during the night, I'm right outside your door." His voice sounded strained, unhappy.

She sat up, but he was gone before she could ask what was wrong.

Her body dropped back onto the bed and her eyes grew heavy. She welcomed the thought of dreaming of the man beyond the door, but instead she faced the nightmare of her childhood.

A loud pounding sound frightened her and she held her crying sister all the tighter. Her father paced in front of the door, mumbling to himself.

Screams sounded from the other side, muffled and distant. She whimpered and rocked. The pounding continued louder and her father yelled.

He rushed over and ushered them under the bed. His lips moved, but she couldn't make out his words. She huddled under the bed with her sister and watched through the gap between the floor and bed skirt. A crack sounded. Her father raced to the door and yelled. "Calm down. I'm coming out."

The lock clicked. The door burst open.

Sara bolted upright, still in the room from her dreams. Only the yellowing curtains and layers of dust told her it was no longer a dream. She shivered, yet felt hot and sweaty at the same time. Pepper moaned and nudged her with his muzzle. White breath plumed in front of her face. It had to be near freezing in the room. She shivered and wrapped the covers tight around her. The moonlight shone through the window, splashing pale light onto the door. She stared at the wood and spotted a crack that ran down the middle. Had her dream been a memory?

Pepper hopped down and clawed at the door, barking. She wrapped the quilt around her and checked her watch. Three in the morning. Her body trembled, an achy cold taking over her limbs and stiffening her toes and fingers. She opened the door to a rush of heat from the fire that still burned strong. Dalton must've put a log on it recently and kept it going throughout the night.

Pepper darted from the bedroom to the front door and barked.

"You need to go out?" Dalton asked Pepper.

Pepper shuffled back a few steps and whined. Dalton stood up, wearing only a thin T-shirt that didn't hide his muscular frame and sweatpants that hung low on his hips. His body glowed in the light of the fire and a hint of inner warmth ignited within her, but her breath remained blue white.

Pepper danced nervously over to where Sara stood in the bedroom doorway, shivering.

Dalton rushed over to her with a furrowed brow. "Whoa, it's frigid in there." He placed a palm on each of her cheeks then swooped her up and hurried to the living room.

"I c-can walk, you know. Is th-this a fireman thing?" Her teeth chattered and she couldn't stop her limbs from shaking.

"You're clammy. Why didn't you come tell me how cold it was in there?" Dalton grabbed his blankets and wrapped her in a cocoon then slid his hands underneath to rub her arms.

"I d-didn't realize how c-cold it was until I woke up." She fought to get control over her body again.

"Sit here. I'll be right back." He threw another log on the fire and it exploded to life once more. Pots clanked around in the kitchen and she heard a burner on the gas stove click on.

"I didn't realize how cold it was because the fire kept me warm. I'm so sorry," he said in a deep, raspy middle-of-the-night sexy tone.

She wasn't sure if it was the fire or his voice, but her shaking eased to more of a tremble. Different hues of gold and red flickered in front of her and she thought about her dream. The sound of the door cracking echoed in her head, as if a distant memory instead of a dream. Had her mother been so violent before her surgery? If so, why would her father leave her and her sister behind and take off?

"Here." Dalton's strong hand held a steaming mug of water with the label from a tea bag hanging out. "I hope you like chamomile. I found it in the cupboard. Hopefully it still has some flavor left."

"Th-thank you."

He sat behind her and rubbed her arms again. "Getting warmed up some?"

"Yeah. I'm much b-better. Thank you." She stared at the liquid as she dipped the tea bag in a few times.

Dalton shimmied around so he sat with his back to the couch and a leg around each side of her. "By that look on your face, that must've been some dream."

She froze then nodded slowly. "I'm not sure if it was a dream or a memory. I think I've blocked that night out for so many years that I'm not clear on what's reality and what's dream."

"What did you dream about?" he asked while lifting the blanket and checking her fingers, as if she had been burned.

"I heard pounding and screams. My dad told us to hide under the bed."

Dalton's hands stopped rubbing her arm. "Was there a break in?"

She grabbed his hand and held it tight, as if he were her lifeline to reality. "No. I think it was my mother. Based on the letters and my dream, I think my father thought she was crazy. The tumor must've made her angry and violent. The sound of her voice frightened me and I remember thinking a monster was on the other side of the door, not my mother, as if they were two different people."

He tucked her hair behind her head, his fingers grazing her cheek. She leaned into him, wanting comfort, something her mother hadn't given to her. "It sounds like she was sick and your dad must've tried to protect you."

"I thought that, too. But if he wanted to protect my sister and me, why would he leave us behind? If he feared for our safety, why wouldn't he take us with him?"

Dalton scooted her tighter into him, wrapping his strong arms around her and laying a soft kiss to the top of her head. For a moment, she thought she could fall asleep right there in his arms. Safe, relaxed, and happy, unlike her childhood and marriage. This moment, here in the small, cold cabin, she thought she had a glimpse of what real love must feel like. The kind that stories are written about, movies are made of and people say they'd die for. A fantasy for sure. But if this was fantasy, she didn't want reality anymore.

"I'm going to go check the furnace. The pilot light must've gone out. I'll be right back. Don't move from the fire." He stroked her head, brushing her hair from her forehead. "I'm sorry you had such a rough time as a child. No child should have to go through that."

The pain in his eyes drew her deeper into the fantasy. A fantasy of a loving marriage and children. He'd be an amazing father. Attentive, loving, protective...like her own father. At least, that was how she remembered him in her dream.

Dalton tightened the blanket around her and left the room. She heard banging and a few choice words before he returned. "I'm afraid we've got a problem. That furnace is dead. It'll have to be replaced. I'm not sure it's worked for years."

He laid blankets from her bedroom and the couch on the floor in front of the fire. "We'll sleep here by the fire so we'll stay warm the rest of the night. Tomorrow,

I'll see if the roads are passable at all. If they are, we can head down the mountain," he said with a distant tone in his voice.

He plopped several pillows down then covered himself with a blanket and curled her into his side. The foreign feeling of sleeping in someone's arms made her pause for a second, but then her body relaxed into him as if they'd slept together for years. Jack had always barricaded her at night, keeping body pillows between them so they didn't touch.

Dalton didn't move, or relax into her the way she did.

"If this is making you uncomfortable, I can sleep on the couch."

"No." He tugged her closer and shimmied down a little so their faces met. "I was worried about making you uncomfortable."

She snickered. "Nope, I'm just fine. This is...nice."

He continued to look at her, as if scanning her face for an answer to an unasked question.

"What?"

Dalton pressed his lips together in an I'm-not-sure-I-should-say-this line.

"Go ahead. Safe zone, remember?" She winked, trying to make him more at ease.

His lips curled into a half-smile. "I didn't want to make you uncomfortable again."

"You haven't made me feel uncomfortable." She tilted her head back a little so she could see his entire face, taking in his firm brow, strong jaw, and sexy dark stubble.

His gaze dropped. "When I kissed you earlier, you pulled away. I'm sorry if I overstepped. I haven't wanted to kiss anyone for a long time and I guess I just—"

Sara cupped his face and pressed her lips to his.

CHAPTER EIGHT

The fire embers glowed, competing with the early morning sunlight that spilled through the glass and spread across the floor. Dalton had never been so thankful for a busted furnace, bad weather, and a drafty old cabin. At this moment, he thanked the Lord for their forced closeness. The way Sara's hair smelled, her soft skin, the warmth of her body next to his made for the best Christmas morning ever.

He ignored the tightness in his back and held perfectly still, not wanting to wake her. If she did, they'd have to separate. For hours, he watched her sleep and listened to Pepper's snoring at their feet. He found an interesting birthmark at her hairline behind her ear, liked the way one eyebrow extended a millimeter further than the other, the fullness of her lips. He studied it all. Each mark or line a detail in the beautiful story of her life. He couldn't contain himself any longer and lightly traced the pale pink circle behind her ear. She stirred and squirmed until her eyes opened, the blueness brighter than the sun and fire combined.

"Good morning," she rasped in a sexy, alluring tone.

He traced from her ear down her jaw line to her chin, her face a perfect heart shape. "Good morning and Merry Christmas."

Pepper stuck his head up and barked.

Sara crawled to the end of their makeshift bed and patted Pepper on the head. "To you, too."

Darn dog. He got all the attention. With a sigh of defeat, he rose and made coffee. "I'll check the weather, but I don't think the roads will be clear until tomorrow. I'm afraid I can't fix that furnace, either." He tried to keep the happiness from his voice, but he knew he'd failed by the way she quirked her head at him and gave a Sherlock Holmes knowing smile.

"I guess we'll just need to sleep by the fire again tonight." She winked.

He fumbled with the coffee lid. Grounds flew all over the counter and floor. What was this girl doing to him? He'd never been so clumsy. She covered her mouth with the back of her hand, but he still heard her giggle.

"You think that was funny?" He rounded the counter.

She burst into laughter and nodded.

"Do you know what I used to do to my sister when she got the best of me?"

She scooted back, as if Pepper would save her, but shook her head.

"I used to tickle her until she cried *mercy.*"

Her eyes shot wide.

"Are you ticklish, Ms. Foster?"

She shook her head, but the way she drew her bottom lip between her teeth gave her away.

He crouched, approaching slowly, taunting her. She held her knees in front of her like a shield, but it didn't do any good. Pepper bolted and slumped to the corner.

"Hey, you're supposed to protect me. I thought we were buddies," Sara called after him.

"He's fickle that way," Dalton teased. "So, you thought that was funny, did you? You like to distract me with that playful wink of yours."

"I didn't mean to. I take it back." Sara held her hands up, but he reached around and planted his hands on her ribs. She remained frozen, her full lips parted as if about to say something, but didn't.

He squeezed and she bucked under his intrusion.

"Wait, no. Okay, I admit it. I'm ticklish."

The wiggles and squirms of her body were nothing in comparison to his strength, but he didn't want to harm her, so he gently rolled her onto her back and leaned on his elbows one on either side of her head. "Good. I know something else about you. I now have a weapon against your womanly wiles."

"Me? Womanly wiles? You give me far too much credit. Besides, you know more about me than my own sister." Her mouth shut and her face tensed, as if she was building the Hoover Dam between them.

"Stop," he said.

Her gaze snapped back to his, the image that plagued her now gone. "Stop what?"

"Building that wall. It's okay that we know a lot about each other. We both agreed, remember?"

Her body relaxed and for a moment, he saw through that façade to a beautiful, open, sexy, loving, and giving woman. One like no other he'd ever met. The way her hair fell by her side in a cascade of shinny strands and the way she pulled her lip between her teeth, he thought she'd undo him right there.

"What?" she muttered.

"You're beautiful."

She tensed for a second, and he didn't know if she didn't handle compliments well or if he'd made her uncomfortable.

She freed a hand and placed her delicate palm to his cheek. "Well, I'd tell you that you are the most handsome, strong, and giving man I'd ever met, but I wouldn't want it going to your head. I mean, I'm sure you're used to women throwing themselves at you."

"Not quality women. Not women who make me spill coffee grounds all over the kitchen," he teased. Her thumb brushed against his jaw, sending his gut tumbling down the mountainside.

He wanted to kiss her. Not the sweet brush of lips they'd shared last night, but a real kiss. The kind that bonded two people in an entirely new way. Did he dare push her, or would she run like a scared doe?

She guided his face closer to hers and slid her hand behind his neck. His pulse raced, hammering so loud he thought it would give him a concussion.

Their lips inches away, the cabin phone shrilled and they both jumped. She retreated and he wanted to go hunting for the person on the other end of that line. If it was Nick, he'd kill him for sure.

He relinquished his hold on her and she padded to the phone. "Sorry, but I gave my ex this number so I could talk to my son this morning. I've never been away from Josh on Christmas before."

Yep, he wouldn't mind a license to hunt ex-husbands. There had to be a season for it somewhere. Of course, he was someone's ex, too.

He shook off his irritation and cleaned the coffee grounds from the counter and floor, all while attempting not to eavesdrop on her conversation, but it was difficult in a small cabin. Whoever was on the other end of the conversation sounded like a cartoon character with muffled words, but Sara's tone indicated they were upsetting her. If it was her ex, Dalton didn't have to know the man to dislike him. Based on what Nick had told him and what Sara had shared, he'd already formed an opinion, and it wasn't a good one.

"What do you mean he's busy? It's Christmas morning and I want to talk to him." Sara's voice hitched.

Dalton continued to clean up and even went to tinker with the furnace he knew would never work again.

"Yes, I'm going to be there for New Year's. I'm not going any longer without seeing Josh. Now, let me talk to him."

New Year's? Deep down, he knew they'd be parting in another day, but part of him hoped they'd meet up in Riverbend for the New Year. Perhaps attend dinner with Nick and her sister after all.

What was he thinking? He'd known this girl for less than twenty-four hours, but what a day it had been.

His heart nearly felt whole again for the first time in years. He could hear her beautiful, lyrical voice and it soothed him like listening to a mellow jazz tune.

"Yes, I'll start driving up as soon as the roads clear, sweetie. I'm sorry you didn't enjoy Christmas, but next year, we can be together and it'll be the best Christmas ever. Don't cry, baby. I'll be there soon. I miss you, too."

She sniffled and he had to fight the urge to go comfort her, but this wasn't any of his business.

"Listen, I don't care if you take me back to court. I'm going to be with my son in the future for Christmas. I don't care if it's in New York or here, but you can't keep us apart. I'm not sure what I was thinking."

Dalton tore himself away and went to scrub his hands clean of old cob webs and rust from the radiator and then returned to the bedroom.

"You're right. I do sound different. And yes, I am going to talk to you this way if it means what's best for Josh. I'm not playing games anymore. Now, you go spend time with Josh instead of dumping him with a sitter. It's Christmas, for God's sake. I'll be there in a few days. But let me make something plain to you. I'm coming up to get my son and that's it. There's no chance of our reconciliation now or ever."

The phone hung up and Dalton hurried into the living room, his arms open and ready for her to cry on his shoulder, but she didn't. Instead, her face was brighter than the Christmas tree in Times Square. She hadn't lost it, had she? He couldn't imagine her throwing pots or pans or knives like Nicole usually did when she got angry.

"I can't believe I did that." She clapped her hands together once. The noise startled Pepper to attention.

Dalton placed his hands on the kitchen counter and slipped onto a stool. "What did you do?"

"I told him it was over. Done. *Finito*, and any other cliché word I can think of to describe the signed, sealed, and delivered rejection gram. My sister's going to be over the moon." She laughed and twirled around the kitchen.

The flow of her hair, the joy filling the room, the happy wave of her arms intoxicated him. "That's good?"

She halted mid-twirl. "Good? It's amazing. I mean, all this time I've tried to reconcile with him for the sake of Josh, but I realized something while I was on the phone with my son. You know what that is?"

Dalton shook his head, not sure what to say.

"That my son isn't happy either. That his father doesn't make him happy. That as a married couple we wouldn't make him happy. I was trying to make things work with Jack because I thought I was abandoning Josh like my father abandoned me, but it's not the same thing. I know it sounds strange, but I think my father didn't want to leave us. I know I don't have any proof. Heck, I'm probably kidding myself." Her voice lowered an octave, sounding strained.

"No, it's your father. And based on those letters he loved you very much. How couldn't he? You must've been an amazing daughter. You're definitely an amazing woman. And you can't feel like you've abandoned Josh because your marriage didn't work.

Staying together with someone you don't love makes life miserable for all those involved."

She nodded. "I know. I just dreamed of having a family one day. One with a happily-ever-after, but I guess that's just in fairy tales."

He left the stool and rounded the counter. "I dreamed of the same thing, but it wasn't meant for me to have a child. I keep praying someday I might be able to adopt, because I believe that if I can't have a happily-ever-after with my own child, I can provide one for someone else's."

The lights flickered a few times, but remained on. Sara glanced at the overhead fixture. "Perhaps my dad is trying to tell me something after all."

"I bet he is. He's telling you to not waste your life on someone you don't love and that you should allow yourself to enjoy life again."

Sara lowered her head to his shoulder. The lights flickered once more and he worried the ice on the power lines would take out the electricity. As much as the idea of snuggling up in front of the fire during a blackout sounded nice, he worried about being cut off in the event of an emergency. "I think we should eat an early Christmas meal. Why don't you go relax and take a hot bath while I make breakfast? I'm afraid it won't be anything too fancy though."

She rose up to her tiptoes and kissed his cheek, sending an excitement comparable to his first kiss with Rebecca Markhem behind the school in fifth grade.

"I still wish I understood why my father left that night. I mean, why would a man leave his two little girls with a woman he thought was going insane?"

Not sure what to say, Dalton remained silent but resolved in that moment to try to find out for her. To help her understand her past, in the hope she'd be open to a better future. Of course, he couldn't give it to her if she wanted more children, but he didn't care. If he could help her, he had to.

"I guess I'll go take that bath before the lights go out. I'll be back in a bit to help with dinner." She slipped from his arms, taking with her the warmth he longed for. Not just from the damp cold of a cabin with no heat, but from the damp cold of life.

He waited until he heard the bathroom door click shut then snagged his cell phone from the kitchen counter. After scrolling through his list of contacts, he picked up the kitchen phone and dialed his friend from Sweetwater County, Sheriff Mason.

"Hello?" Jimmy's deep voice boomed.

"Hi, bud. It's Dalton. How are you?"

"Fine, fine. Merry Christmas to you, good buddy."

"Merry Christmas. How's that new wife of yours?"

Jimmy chuckled. "Barefoot and pregnant."

Dalton heard a woman's voice scolding in the distance, but he couldn't make out the words. "I'm afraid I'm not just calling to wish you a merry Christmas. I need a favor."

"Ah, I thought so. What can I do for the guy who saved my life?"

"Stop that. That happened so long ago, it doesn't even count anymore." Dalton bent down and stroked Pepper's forehead.

"But if you hadn't covered for me that night, I wouldn't be a police officer today. I'm still glad you were underage and only got a slap on the wrist."

"Yeah, well, you probably saved me, too. I never had much time for teenage pranks after that night."

They both laughed at the memory of their wayward teen years.

"So, whatcha need?"

If he remembered correctly, Nick had told him that Sara was twenty-eight. If she was five when her dad died. "I want to know if you can pull a file from 1992. It's only a hunch, but I think there was a domestic dispute call at the cabin I'm staying at back on Christmas Eve of that year. It was the same night as a car accident on the Black Ice Bridge that resulted in a fatality."

"Hmm...I think I have some connections up in the Smokeys. I'll see what I can do."

"Thanks. I know it'll take a few days with the holidays and everything, but as soon as you can get me the information would be great."

"Done. And Dalton?"

"Yeah?"

"I hope she's worth it." The phone clicked off, leaving Dalton to wonder how Jimmy knew this had to do with a woman.

CHAPTER NINE

The room was silent, but no words needed to be spoken. A magical evening of brief touches and almost kisses nearly drove Sara mad with desire. Not just physical desire, but mental. That deep emotional connection where you long to tell someone how you feel, even though you know it's too soon. Way too soon in the case of Dalton Scott.

His hand brushed the hair from her face and he rested his chin on the top of her head. "It's not so bad with no heat or lights."

The room glowed with orange and yellow hues while white snow floated down outside the window. The lights no longer even flickered in an attempt to turn on. "Nope. Not bad at all."

Quilts from yesteryears surrounded their entwined bodies, keeping them warm while they rested together and she dreamed of tomorrow. *Tomorrow?* Despite the warmth, she stiffened. What would tomorrow bring? If the weather warmed up and melted the ice as predicted, it would end their time together. What then? Would she ever see him again? She longed to get to New York to get Josh, but she could fly up and bring him back to Riverbend in time to spend New Year's at home. Screw what Jack wanted. She'd wasted years of her life worrying about that jerk. It was time for her to get what she wanted.

Dalton twitched and his breathing slowed. His chin drifted off her head so she looked up to watch this rock of a man next to her. He still looked manly, yet fragile as he slept. His eyebrow arched, his mouth twitched and she wondered what he dreamed of? He mumbled something, but she couldn't make it out. He twitched several more times before she laced her arm around his middle and snuggled back into his side. He settled and she fought her own heavy eyes. The thought of waking to the day they'd be parting weighed on her heart like a fallen tree pinning her to the ground.

Life-like dreams claimed her for the night. Her father stood at the doorway. The sound of a struggle then something clinked to the floor. Her baby sister began to cry, but Sara put her hand over her mouth, without blocking her nose the way her dad had shown her.

A scream. A door slammed.

She bolted upright, her heart beating against her ribs. Her sweatshirt and yoga pants clung to her soaked skin. The dream, only a breath away, faded as her heartbeat slowed. Was it a memory? Did something happen that night that she couldn't remember? Her aunt had always told her she was too young and that was why she couldn't recall much from the night her dad died. But now, she wasn't so sure.

Sara took long, cleansing breaths and kept the covers low on her hips while attempting not to wake Dalton.

It was sometime in the early morning hours that she woke again to Dalton tossing another log on the fire. His shirt pulled tight across his wide shoulders with each movement and she yearned for him to return to her side.

"Can't sleep?"

Dalton snuggled back next to her and tucked her into his side. "Just checking the fire." Pepper nudged onto the foot of their makeshift bed until he rested his head on her foot.

"Now, go back to sleep. Sweet dreams," Dalton whispered in her ear.

She fought to remain awake, but her body gave in to the night's call just as she heard something more. Terms of endearment from a man she found to be everything she'd ever desired. Or was it all a dream?

Warm rays caressed her face and she blinked against the bright light. She stretched and found the spot on the blankets next to her vacant, only his woodsy aroma left behind. She bolted upright and scanned the room. No sign of him, but the dim light from the table lamp indicated the electricity was back on. She stood and twisted in the quilt to look around, but still nothing. A sound outside the window drew her attention and she shuffled over to the bright light. Outside, she found Dalton shoveling snow.

The cabin phone rang with a hair-raising shrill and she bolted to the kitchen to answer it. "Hello?"

"Hello? Sara?" Her sister's voice came over the line like a beacon of light ready to guide her through the dark woods.

"Hi. How was your Christmas?" *Start with small talk.* She was going to need a moment before she could bring up the real reason she wanted to talk to her sister.

"It was great, but it would've been even better if you were here. I tried to call last night, but the lines were down. I didn't know about Dalton being there, I swear. I didn't find out until we were on the phone when you were headed up the mountain."

"Don't worry about it." Sara walked as far as the cord on the phone would allow. But it was enough for her to catch glimpses of Dalton as he stood then dug the shovel into the snow, over and over again. The man was strong.

"What? You're not going to scold me?" Susan chuckled. "Wow. You must've had a *good* Christmas."

"It was nice." She sighed. "It was really nice."

"Huh? Am I talking to Sara? Or did some mountain lion eat her up and spit someone else out?"

"There aren't any mountain lions around here. Well, I don't think so anyway. Bears maybe,"
she teased.

"Was that a joke? Okay, spill it, sis. Something's definitely going on."

There was a long pause. What could she say? Eyeing the man beyond the window made her heart flutter and her head feel light?

"Oh my god! You like Dalton. I knew it. I told you he was everything any girl would ever dream of having. Not to mention he loves kids. Nick says he could have any woman he wants but shows little interest. He's apparently down-to-earth and not a dog. A rare creature."

"Yes, he's all of those things."

Her sister huffed. "I know that tone. What is it? His hair's combed the wrong way? Or is it that you're still clinging to that worthless ex of yours—"

"No. I'm done with Jack. I told him yesterday there'd be no reconciling. I came to the realization that life for Josh is better with us apart than together. I thought I had to give him a full-time mother and father for him to have a good life, but I realized I can't force that. He's never happy when we're all together and he certainly isn't happy being with his father for Christmas."

"Great. Then what's the problem? Dalton's pants sit too low on his butt? What excuse do you have this time?" Her sister sounded exasperated.

"You know, *I'm* supposed to be the big sister. I'm supposed to take care of you. Stop worrying about me. I'm fine."

"You've been taking care of me my entire life. It's my turn. Now, tell me. What is it? I can hear that flight sound in your voice."

"It's not me. I mean, I'm not sure what's between Dalton and me, but I know I want to find out."

"Then stay at the cabin, figure it out."

Pepper trotted up to her side as if to agree with her sister. "I need to get Josh from New York. He's miserable and I can't be happy if he's suffering."

"I'll buy you a round trip ticket. I'll even take you to the airport and pick you up. You can be back the same day and I'll hang with Josh. I'd love to spend time with my nephew. And he needs a mom who's healthy and happy."

"I thought about flying up, but I doubt I'll be able to get a flight. Not with it being the holidays. Besides, it's not me that doesn't want to stay." Tears welled in Sara's eyes.

"Oh. Sara, are you sure? I don't believe that. He has to like you. Why wouldn't he?"

"He does. I'm almost positive he feels the same way I do, but..."

"But what?" Susan asked, her voice reducing to a motherly tone.

"I woke up this morning and he was gone. He's out there digging my car out of the snow so I can leave. That doesn't sound like a man who wants to spend any more time with me."

"You don't know that. Now, you listen to me. I can still hear that thing in your voice. The one that keeps men a few steps away at all times. If he's out there digging your car out, it's because he doesn't know how *you* feel. You've probably kept him just far enough away to alienate his affection. Get out there and tell him how you feel."

"I've only known him for two days. Even I don't know how I feel."

"Two solid days trapped in a cabin. That's gotta equal time enough for like ten dates. So, really you've been dating over two months already."

"You never were too good at math, were you?" Sara teased, trying to lighten the mood.

"No more deflecting and trying to avoid whatever might be good in your life. I know you went up to that cabin to face some sort of childhood problem. I'm sorry I was too young to remember what happened. Perhaps if we had both been babies when Dad died you wouldn't have this issue with men. But whatever it is, you need to deal with it before you lose someone amazing, unless there *is* something wrong with him."

Dalton set the shovel down and wiped snow from her car windshield. "No. He's attentive, loving, strong, confident, vulnerable, funny, smart, and gorgeous."

"Leave anything out?" her sister teased. "For goodness sake, girl, go get him. Or you'll regret it for the rest of your life."

"Can we do New Year's at your place? I think I'd like that date after all."

"Abso-tively!"

Sara chuckled then took a long cleansing breath. She'd never told a man how she felt before, not truly. She and Jack had said *I love you*, but it always felt like an obligation, something expected as opposed to a true emotion. Thinking back, their entire relationship never had contained passion and emotion. It was mechanical, like a business contract. That was, until she grew tired of him spending all her money. Dalton was real, and he stood only feet away. She could do this. What did she have to lose?

Saying goodbye, she hung up then shoved her feet into her boots, put on her coat, and marched out the front door. The bitter wind burned her nose and cheeks, the smell of wood smoke mixed with pine trees invigorating her. She shuffled around the car and stopped a few feet away from Dalton, waiting for him to wrap his arms around her and pull her close like he'd done so often in the last two days, but he didn't. Instead, he turned away and walked to the other side of the car.

Her chest tightened and she froze to the spot, unsure what to say or do. Perhaps her sister was right, she needed to go for it. To put herself out there and tell him how she felt. To show him that she was ready to let go of the past and focus on the future.

She rounded the car, stopping beside him, and helped him with the snow. "Good morning."

"Good morning. Did you sleep okay?" He abandoned the car and her for the shovel.

The tightness in her chest constricted the air in her lungs. "Fine. You?"

"Good. I thought I should get up and start shoveling. Turns out there's more weather coming. If you're gonna make it off this mountain anytime soon, you're only going to have a few hours between when the ice melts and refreezes."

They could've been snowed in another few days here, but he chose to make sure that didn't happen. The constriction turned into an iron clamp on her heart, squeezing until she thought she'd collapse in the snow. He wanted to leave, not stay with her.

No, she wouldn't give up that easy. These were just words. She needed to touch him, to show him that she was all in.

With a determined step, she marched through the snow to him. His gaze snapped to her and for a brief second, she swore he looked like a bear caught in headlights. A small baby black bear that didn't know if he should attack or run.

He spun on his heels, nearly falling in the snow, and ran. Ran away from her arms, from their weekend, from any possibility of tomorrow.

CHAPTER TEN

Dalton stomped the snow from his boots, trying to shake the ache from his heart as well. He couldn't touch Sara or he'd never be able to let her go. And he had to. She had a son, and if he had a child, there would be nothing to stand in the way of him getting to his little one during the holidays, especially after that phone call last night.

He opened the door, removed his gloves and coat, and shoved his hands in his pocket. "I'll make some hot chocolate. Why don't you sit by the fire? It'll be another hour or two before the roads clear enough for you to drive."

Sara hung her coat on the wall hook and tended the fire. Pepper whined and plopped down by her side, as if he knew she'd be gone soon. The aroma of hot chocolate didn't sooth his raw nerves as he'd hoped. With a heavy step, he crossed the room and handed her a mug. Her pinky grazed his finger. The shock he'd felt at their first touch, and every touch since, ignited his desire to beg her to stay.

No, he had to let her go. Instead of sitting by her side and torturing himself with her inviting fragrance and soft full lips, he returned to the kitchen and busied himself with washing the spoon and pot.

"I'm going to get dressed and get ready to head out," she said with a sadness in the tone of her voice. Before he could ask her what was wrong, she closed the bedroom door.

The phone rang twice, so he answered. Part of him hoped it was her ex, so he could give him a piece of his mind.

"Hey, man. How's it going?" Nick asked.

"Fine." Dalton leaned against the kitchen counter. "Hey, you think that wife of yours can host New Year's Eve? You guys tried so hard to set up Sara and me, now's your chance to see it through."

"You want to see her again? That's great. Sure. I can make that happen. Actually, she already told me you and Sara would be here. Susan called Sara a bit ago and she asked the same thing."

"Really?" The hope in his voice made him cringe. He'd never heard his own voice sound so desperate. But he *was* desperate. Desperate to feel her in his arms again and never let her go. And after she returned with Josh, and he knew that her ex was out of the picture for good, that was what he'd do.

"Yeah. Why don't you guys just stay up there? Or you can return to Riverbend and hang together. You don't have to be back on shift until the day after New Year's, right?"

"Yeah, but she has to go to New York. I think I'm gonna pick up a few shifts in the meantime. I'm afraid there's little I can do for your cabin until we get some parts in. A new furnace for one thing, and supplies for a new roof."

"Geesh. That bad?"

"Yep. It'll take months before this place is ready to sell."

"Gotcha. Thanks for checking it out, man. Susan was adamant she wanted that place gone as soon as possible, something about her sister having nightmares about that place. She wasn't happy at all when she found out Sara was going there. Said it was some sort of punishment to herself for her failed marriage."

Dalton thought back over their conversations and what they'd learned about each other. It had to be rough on anyone thinking his or her father abandoned them then died before he could explain. He wasn't sure Sara would ever heal without knowing the entire story. "That explains a lot."

"Glad it does to you. I'm afraid I don't speak Venus."

"Venus?"

Nick laughed. "Yeah, something Susan told me once. Apparently, I'm from another planet."

The door to the bedroom opened so he quickly ended the call and smiled. Sara didn't even look at him. Instead she returned her attention to Pepper.

"Guess it's my turn. I'll go grab a shower and get dressed then we can check the roads. The ice should be melting pretty quickly, and I think I heard salt trucks out on the mountain road."

She only nodded. With a sigh, he hopped in the shower and cleaned up. A quick towel dry and he grabbed his clothes.

A car starting echoed through the small cabin from outside. He looked around and saw Sara's stuff still on the bed. It couldn't be her. Perhaps there was a cabin nearby he wasn't aware of.

He hurried to the living room, only to find Pepper scratching at the front door. He opened and peered out to catch a glimpse of tail lights headed down the drive. What was she doing? She had to get out of here so badly that she left without saying goodbye?

He quickly put on his boots and coat. Before he could rush out the door, the phone rang. He debated about ignoring it, but thinking it might be Nick again, he picked it up.

"Hello?"

"Hey, man. I've got some information for you." Jimmy's voice sounded from the other end of the phone.

"That was fast."

"I remembered my contact, a man that I worked for right out of the academy. I called him this morning and discovered he was on duty that night. He was the first officer on the scene. Turns out the mother was taken away in an ambulance. When the police arrived she was in an unstable mental state. She'd locked herself inside the bedroom, screaming about killing her babies if the devil got any closer. They only found her because the husband wrecked his car while trying to get help. Before he passed, he told my friend that his wife was ill and that she needed help before she killed his children. Phone lines were down that night, so he probably had to race down the mountain in order to get any help."

So Sara's father didn't abandon her. He had tried to save her.

"Thank you. You have no idea what this means. Listen, I'll treat you to dinner after the holidays as a thank you. Send my regards to Trianna. I've got to go."

"I'm glad I could help."

Dalton bolted out of the cabin to his car. Pepper raced after him, but when he opened the passenger side door, Pepper didn't get in. Instead the dog raced past him down the hill, barking.

"Pepper, come back!" He looked down at the snow-covered tires and swore under his breath. He didn't have time to dig his car out. With bare hands, he tugged at the buildup of ice behind his wheels, and to his relief the chunk popped free. The snow and ice had already started melting.

He started his jeep and rocked it back and forth until he could find traction and the wheels broke free. He had to find Sara. Despite what he feared, he couldn't let her go. If he had to follow her all the way to New York just to be with her, he would. Forget the ex, the jerk didn't deserve her. But still, was it right for him to ask her to be with him if he couldn't give her more children? He had to find out.

CHAPTER ELEVEN

The roads were still slick, but passable. Sara took it slow, swiping at the tears that streamed from her eyes. She couldn't spend another moment in the cabin with Dalton being so distant. She couldn't face his rejection. It was obvious they'd had a great weekend. They'd helped each other through some things, but now it was over. That was all it was to him, a weekend of therapy.

Now she needed to move on. Not return to Jack, but to open her heart to future possibilities. Yet, her heart remained on that mountain no matter how fast she traveled away from the cabin.

A patch of black ice sent her tires into a frenzy. The traction control light flashed before her car skidded then recovered. Avoiding the brakes and gas as much as possible, she crawled down the drive and onto the main road. To her relief the road had been salted, so the drive back into town wouldn't be as treacherous as she had feared.

If it had been, she would've just waited it out at the bottom of the drive, far away from Dalton's rejection, but still safe. After all, she wouldn't risk her life the way her father had. She had a child to get home to. Feelings of anger bubbled up and she hit the steering wheel with the palm of her hand. "Why'd you abandon us?"

Only the sound of crunching sand and salt answered. She rounded the corner and the bridge came into view. The one her father had lost control on. She slowed to a stop and eyed her nemesis. It was salted and tire tracts through the snow told her it was passable, so she edged forward. A lump lodged in her throat. She looked up the mountain and caught a glimpse of the cabin's roof. He'd died so close to them. She forced her gaze back to the path in front of her and caught sight of something dark struggling on the side of the hill next to the bridge.

A bear? No, it was too small. She slowed and eyed the creature until she got close enough to see. "Pepper?"

She pulled off to the side of the road just short of the bridge and went to get a closer look. Sure enough, Pepper struggled only a few feet away from the edge of the road. With slow determined steps, she approached the embankment and sank to her knees. "What are you doing out here?" she asked. Pepper clawed and scurried on the side of the hill. "Come on, boy. You can do it."

Pepper slipped a few inches further. Sara scooted to the edge, braced one foot against the railing and the other on a rock below and reached for Pepper. His nails dug into her skin, but she managed to catch him around his waist and lift him to her side. He clawed over her shoulder and jumped free of the embankment. She turned, but her foot slipped, causing her legs to separate further. Snow and ice pummeled down the side of the mountain and her foot continued to follow. She grabbed the edge of a rock with one hand and swung her leg off the railing so she could crawl back up. But there was nothing to support her below. She kicked and flailed, trying to find something, anything to leverage her feet on to keep her from sliding down the mountain.

Pepper howled and barked from the side of the road.

She swung her other arm up and grabbed the railing, but something pierced her skin and her hand let go instinctively.

Car tires racing over sand and ice sounded beyond her hammering pulse in her ears.

"Help! Help me! I'm down here." She struggled to keep hold of the slick rock, but her fingers were losing feeling the colder they got. She waited for that adrenaline rush everyone spoke of when you were facing death, but no extra energy pumped into her frozen limbs.

"Dear God, please don't let my son grow up without me," she whispered. Tears streamed down her face. Blood gushed from her palm. Her heart pumped.

A hand grabbed her wrist. "I've got you."

Her fingers slipped from the rock. "Don't let go!"

With one heave, she landed back on the road and fell into her savior's arms.

"I'll never let go," Dalton rasped in her ear, wrapping his arms tight around her.

She shook and cried as he lifted her into his lap and held her until her heart slowed and she could breathe again.

"You're hurt." He took off his coat then his flannel shirt and wrapped it around her hand before putting his coat back on and lifting her from the ground. "Come on. We need to get you warm." He carried her to her car and cranked the heat to high. "Why'd you leave like that?" Dalton asked while rubbing life back into her arms.

"I-I thought you wanted me to go. That we'd had our weekend and it was time to move on. But I wasn't strong enough to face the goodbye."

"Why would you think that?" He cupped her cheeks, his hand and eyes caressing her with his undivided attention. The way only Dalton could do.

"You were so distant. I tried to talk to you, but you kept walking away from me." She swallowed the boulder-sized lump blocking her throat and forced herself to continue. "I thought you enjoyed the weekend, but that's all it was to you. A therapy session."

"No. I'm such an idiot. I'm sorry. I didn't realize." He leaned back and ran a hand through his thick hair. "I wasn't done with the weekend. I didn't want you to leave, but I didn't want to stand in the way of you and your son either. I knew if I didn't get you out soon, if I touched you one more time, I wouldn't be able to let you go."

She sucked in a quick breath.

He brushed hair from her eyes then ran a thumb over her bottom lip. "The last thing I want is for us to spend just a weekend together, but you deserve better. You deserve more children and a life of happiness."

"I told you I don't care about more kids. I'm not even sure I should've been a mother. I've mucked up Josh's life with a failed marriage, and gave in to my ex by sending him there for Christmas, the way my father gave up on me all those years ago."

"No, that's not what happened. I called a friend of mine and he contacted someone he knew that was on duty the night your father died. It turns out your mother had some sort of psychotic break. I guess it was related to that tumor, I'm not sure, but your father was racing down the mountain to get help. Your mother had you girls locked in the bedroom with a knife, threatening you both if the devil came near her. The phone lines were down since there was a big storm that night. That's why he had to leave. There was no other way he could save you."

Her breath stuttered, air trapped just inches away from her lungs.

"It's okay, Sara. I'm here and I'm not going anywhere. Your father didn't leave you either. He saved you. He told the officer on scene about your mother before he passed. He saved your life while sacrificing his own. He loved you, Sara."

She broke, heart-sobbing cries racking her body. Cries she'd kept trapped inside for decades poured from her until she couldn't cry any longer. Dalton held her to him, stroking her hair, never judging her for breaking down.

"Th-thank you," she finally managed between half-breaths.

"You haven't failed your son anymore than your father failed you. Now, go and get your son and enjoy him. Someday you can have more kids and a family. You're free to find your happily-ever-after."

"What if I don't want to be free?" She lifted her head to face him. Despite her bawling like a little baby, she knew she had to see his eyes. "What if I want you?"

He closed his eyes, as if memorizing her words, or bracing himself for something. "I can't give you a family. You deserve—"

"You. Because that's all I want. I've never thought about having another child. Even if I did, we could adopt. Please, don't let that keep you from me. I want to spend more time with you. I want to get to know you better, not just here during Christmas, but in everyday life." She straightened and pushed her shoulders back, ready to put it all out there and not hold back. "Unless you don't feel the same. Perhaps it was just a Christmas miracle. We found our way and now you're ready to move—"

He cupped her cheeks and pulled her into him. His lips pressed to hers with such intensity. A kiss filled with hopes, dreams, promises, and love. A kiss that melted her heart and her body into him. A kiss that would be forever remembered. An epic, once-in-a-lifetime kiss.

Unable to breathe, speak, move, Sara closed her eyes and enjoyed every brush and tender caress he gave.

When they parted lips, Dalton rested his head against hers.

"Come with me. If you don't have to work, drive with me to New York and meet Josh. We can drive back and spend the New Year at my sister and Nick's place." Her heart continued to thrash at car-racing speed.

"I'd love that."

Pepper barked.

"You can go with us, too," Sara giggled.

Dalton nodded his agreement.

"You sure about this? You'll go all the way to New York with me? I mean, it could just be that Christmas sparkly new toy syndrome kind of relationship."

Dalton pulled her close once more, their lips only inches apart. "No, it's much more. I get what your father meant about the Christmas spark. You're my Christmas spark. My life spark."

EPILOGUE

Christmas Eve
Two Years Later

J osh bounded through the kitchen, Pepper barking and skating across the floor as he chased after him. "It's time. It's time to light the tree!"

Nick unlatched the high chair, which allowed Noah to escape, toddling after Josh while his other cousin Natalie retrieved her doll from her chair and walked with all the attitude a six-year-old prima donna could manage.

Dalton slid his arm around Sara's shoulders and led her to the main room. "Susan, that was delicious. I see where your sister gets her cooking skills from."

Susan giggled and snuggled into Nick's side. Her belly was plump with her third child, but Dalton didn't feel that twinge of jealousy he usually did at the site of a pregnant woman.

"I hope I cook better than that," Susan laughed.

"Trust me, you do," Sara reassured her.

"You on shift tonight?" Nick asked.

"Nope. I do have to go in tomorrow night, though." Dalton didn't like working holidays. He hated being away from Sara for even one night. He took her left hand in his and kissed her wedding ring. Each day he cherished the fact she'd said *yes*.

Josh plopped down in front of the tree, ready with the cord to plug into the wall.

"I've been considering working more in construction and quitting the fire department. I love what I do, but if I did contract work I could be home every night."

Josh dropped the cord and hurtled over the presents into Dalton's arms. The little man had become his own son. He only hoped he lived up to the part. After his father found out he wouldn't be able to bleed any more money out of Sara, he'd disappeared, only calling once or twice a year. How could any man turn his back on his child?

"That would be awesome." Josh squeezed tight.

Sara smiled up at him. "You sure about that? I You're a great fireman and I don't want you to give that up just because you think it's the right thing to do."

"No. It's what I want." Dalton kissed her forehead. Even after a year and a half of marriage, he couldn't stop touching his beautiful wife. He felt whole, his life finally complete.

"Well, I think that's great. Sara won't admit it, but she worries each time you're on shift," Susan chimed in, offering her opinion as always.

"Well, now she won't have to worry." Dalton rustled Josh's hair. "Why don't you go light that Christmas tree now."

Josh scurried to his place of honor and plugged the lights into the wall. The tree lit up with red and green lights. The ornaments shimmered, reflecting colors onto the nearby wall.

Nick rubbed his hand over Susan's belly and leaned over to speak to the unborn child. "Next year, you'll get to see the Christmas lights."

Sara squeezed Dalton's hand and nodded. Excitement shot through him and he tucked her into his side. It was finally time to share. "That'll be nice, and he'll have a baby cousin to share it with." Dalton rubbed Sara's belly, longing to feel the baby kick. He still didn't know how it could be possible.

"Doctors confirmed last week," Sara said. "Now that we've reached three months and the baby is doing well, we can finally tell people."

"But...I thought..." Susan shot up, knocking Nick aside with her big belly.

"I guess it's a miracle. They said we had a thousand to one shot. Apparently, we should play the lottery," Sara teased and kissed Dalton's cheek.

Josh jumped up and down. "You mean I'm gonna have a little brother?"

"Or sister," Sara added.

"Wow! This is the best Christmas ever!"

"I agree, buddy." Dalton touched Sara's belly once more before Susan swooped in to hug and squeal with her sister.

Nick offered his hand. "Congratulations. I'm so happy for you both."

Susan held her sister in her arms. "I guess you finally found the Christmas spark you were looking for all those years."

Dalton reached out, pulling his bride, his stepson, and his unborn child into his arms. "We found the Christmas fire."

THE END

If you've enjoyed this story please take a second to write a review or tell a friend about what you've read.

For more information please visit
http://www.ciaraknight.com.
Or send her an email at:
ciara@ciaraknight.com

ABOUT THE AUTHOR

Ciara Knight is a USA Today and Amazon Bestselling author who writes 'A Little Edge and A Lot of Heart' that span the heat scales. Her popular sweet romance series, Sweetwater County (rated G), is a small town romance full of family trials, friendly competition, and community love. Also, there is a brand new sister series, Riverbend. The prequel novella is now available on all online retailers, and the first four books will release in 2016.

When not writing, she enjoys reading all types of fiction. Some great literary influences in her life include Edgar Allen Poe, Shakespeare, Francine Rivers and J K Rowling.

Her first love, besides her family, reading, and writing, is travel. She's backpacked through Europe, visited orphanages in China, and landed in a helicopter on a glacier in Alaska.

Ciara is extremely sociable and can be found at Facebook @ciaraknightwrites, Twitter @ciaratknight, Goodreads, Pinterest, and her website ciaraknight.com.

Made in the USA
Charleston, SC
15 November 2015